WITHIN AND WITHOUT

AND

A HIDDEN LIFE

By GEORGE MAC DONALD, LL.D.

LONDON: ALEXANDER STRAHAN
25 HENRIETTA STREET, COVENT GARDEN
1884

CONTENTS.

TO

L. P. M. D.

RECEIVE thine own; for I and it are thine.
Thou know'st its story ; how for forty days
Weary with sickness and with social haze,
(After thy hands and lips with love divine
Had somewhat soothed me, made the glory shine,
Though with a watery lustre,) more delays
Of blessedness forbid—I took my ways
Into a solitude, Invention's mine;
There thought and wrote afar, and yet with thee.
Those days gone past, I came, and brought a book
My child, developed since in limb and look.
It came in shining vapours from the sea,
And in thy stead sung low sweet songs to me,
When the red life-blood labour would not brook.
G. M. D. May, 1855.
VOL, I.

George MacDonald (10 December 1824 – 18 September 1905) was a Scottish author, poet, and Christian minister. He was a pioneering figure in the field of fantasy literature and the mentor of fellow writer Lewis Carroll. His writings have been cited as a major literary influence by many notable authors including W. H. Auden, C. S. Lewis, J. R. R. Tolkien, Walter de la Mare,E. Nesbit and Madeleine L'Engle.C. S. Lewis wrote that he regarded MacDonald as his "master": "Picking up a copy of Phantastes one day at a train-station bookstall, I began to read. A few hours later," said Lewis, "I knew that I had crossed a great frontier." G. K. Chesterton cited The Princess and the Goblin as a book that had "made a difference to my whole existence".Elizabeth Yates wrote of Sir Gibbie, "It moved me the way books did when, as a child, the great gates of literature began to open and first encounters with noble thoughts and utterances were unspeakably thrilling."

Even Mark Twain, who initially disliked MacDonald, became friends with him, and there is some evidence that Twain was influenced by MacDonald. Christian author Oswald Chambers (1874–1917) wrote in Christian Disciplines, vol. 1, (pub. 1934) that "it is a striking indication of the trend and shallowness of the modern reading public that George MacDonald's books have been so neglected".

In addition to his fairy tales, MacDonald wrote several works on Christian apologetics including several that defended his view of Christian Universalism.

WITHIN AND WITHOUT.

PART I.

Go thou into thy closet; shut thy door ;
And pray to Him in secret: He will hear.
But think not thou, by one wild bound, to clear
The numberless ascensions, more and more,
Of starry stairs that must be climbed, before
Thou comest to the Father's likeness near,
And bendest down to kiss the feet so dear
That, step by step, their mounting flights passed o'er.
Be thou content if on thy weary need
There falls a sense of showers and of the spring ;
A hope that makes it possible to fling
Sickness aside, and go and do the deed ;
For highest aspiration will not lead
Unto the calm beyond all questioning.
B

PART I.
SCENE I.—A cell in a convent. JULIAN alone.

JULIAN. Evening again, slow creeping
like a death ! And the red sunbeams fading from
the wall,
On which they flung a sky, with streaks and bars Of the poor window-pane that let them in, For clouds and shadings of the mimic heaven ! Soul of my cell, they part, no more to come. But what is light to me, while I am dark ! And yet they strangely draw me, those faint hues, Reflected flushes from the Evening's face,
Which &s a bride, with glowing arms outstretched, Takes to her blushing heaven him who has left His chamber in the dim deserted east. Through walls and hills I see it ! The rosy sea ! The radiant head half-sunk ! A pool of light, As the blue globe had by a blow been broken, And the insphered glory bubbled forth ! Or the sun were a splendid water-bird, That flying furrowed with its golden feet A flashing wake over the waves, and home ! Lo there !—Alas, the dull blank wall!—High up, The window-pane a dead grey eye ! And night Come on me like a thief!— -'Tis best; the sun Has always made me sad. I'll go and pray : The terror of the night begins with prayer.

(Vesper bell.) Call them that need thee ; I need
not thy summons ;
My knees would not so pain me when I kneel, If only at thy voice my prayer awoke.
SCENE . WITHIN AND WITHOUT.

I will not to the chapel. When I find Him,
Then will I praise him from the heights of peace;
But now my soul is as a speck of life
Cast on the deserts of eternity ;
A hungering and a thirsting, nothing more.
I am as a child new-born, its mother dead,
Its father far away beyond the seas.
Blindly I stretch my arms and seek for him :
He goeth by me, and I see him not.
I cry to him : as if I sprinkled ashes,
My prayers fall back in dust upon my soul.
(Choir and organ-music. I bless you, sweet
sounds, for your visiting. "What friends I have ! Prismatic harmonies Have just departed in the sun's bright car, And fair, convolved sounds troop in to me, Stealing my soul with faint deliciousness. Would they took shapes ! What levees I should
hold !
How should my cell be filled with wavering forms ! Louder they grow, each swelling higher, higher ; Trembling and hesitating to float off, As bright air-bubbles linger, that a boy Blows, with their interchanging, wood dove hues, Just throbbing to their flight, like them to die. — Gone now ! Gone to the Hades of dead loves !
Is it for this that I have left the world ? Left what, poor fool ? Is this, then, all that comes
Of that night when the closing door fell dumb On music and on voices, and I went Forth from the ordered tumult of the dance, Under the clear cope of the moonless night, Wandering away without the city-walls, Between the silent meadows and the stars, Till something woke in me, and moved my spirit, And of themselves my thoughts turned towards
God ;
When straight within my soul I felt as if An eye was opened ; but I knew not whether 'Twas I that saw, or God that looked on me ? It closed again, and darkness fell; but not To hide the memory ; that, in many failings Of spirit and of purpose, still returned ; And I came here at last to search for God. Would I could find him ! Oh, what quiet content Would then absorb my heart, yet leave it free.
A knock at the door. Enter Brother ROBERT with a light.
Robert. Head in your hands as usual! Yc;
will fret
Your life out, sitting moping in the dark. Come, it is supper-time.
Julian. I will not sup to-night.
Robert. Not sup ! You'll never live to be ai saint.
Julian. A saint ! The devil has me by the heel.
Robert. So has he all saints ; as a boy his kite, Which ever struggles higher for his hold. It is a silly devil to gripe so hard ; — He should let go his hold, and then he has you. If you'll not come, I'll leave the light with you. I lark to the chorus ! Brother Stephen sings.
Chorus. Ahuays merry, and never drunk, That's the life of the jolly monk.
SONG.
They say the first monks were lonely men, Praying each in his lonely den, Rising up to kneel again, Each a skinny male Magdalen, Peeping scared from out his hole Like a burrowing

rabbit or a mole ; But years ring changes as they roll.

Cho. Now always merry,

When the moon gets up with her big round face, Like Mistress Poll's in the market-place, Down to the village below we pace ; — We know a supper that wants a grace :

SCENE i. WITHIN AND WITHOUT. «

Past the curtseying women we go,

Past the smithy, all a-glow,

To the snug little houses at top of the row.

Cho. For always merry, &>c.

And there we find, amongst the ale,

The fragments of a floating tale :

To piece them together we never fail;

And we fit them rightly, I'll go bail.

And so we have them all in hand,

The lads and lasses throughout the land,

And we are the masters,—you understand ?

Cho. So always merry, &c.

Last night we had such a game of play

With the nephews and nieces over the way,

All for the gold that belonged to the clay

That lies in lead till the judgment-day.

The old man's soul they'd leave in the lurch ;

But we saved her share for old Mamma Church.

How they eyed the bag as they stood in the porch!

Cho. Oh ! always merry, and never drunk, Thafs the life of the jolly monk!

Robert. The song Is hardly to your taste, I see. Where shall I set the light ?

Julian. I do not need it.

Robert. Come, come ! The dark is a hot-bed

for fancies.

I wish you were at table, were it only To stop the talking of the men about yoa. You in the dark are talked of in the light. Julian. Well, brother, let them talk ; it hurts

not me. Robert. No ; but it hurts your friend to hear

them say,

You would be thought a saint without the trouble. You do no penance that they can discover ; You keep shut up, say some, eating your heart, Possessed with a bad conscience, the worst demon. You are a prince, say others, hiding here, Fill circumstance that bound you, set you free. To-night, there are some whispers of a lady That would refuse your love. Julian. Ay ! What of her ?

Robert. I heard no more than so; and that you

came

To seek the next best service you could find : Turned from the lady's door, and knocked at God's.

Julian. One part at least is true : I knock at

God's;

He has not yet been pleased to let me in. As for the lady—that is—so far true, But matters little. Had I less to do, This talking might annoy me ; as it is, Why, let the wind set there, if it pleases it; I keep in-doors.

Robert. Gloomy as usual, brother !

Brooding on fancy's eggs. God did not send The light that all day long gladdened the earth, Flashed from the snowy peak, and on the spire Transformed the weathercock into a star, That you should gloom within stone walls all day.

At dawn to-morrow, take your staff, and come: We will salute the breezes, as they rise And leave their lofty beds, laden with odours Of melting snow, and fresh damp earth, and
moss;

Imprisoned spirits, which life-waking Spring Lets forth in vapour through the genial air. Come, we will see the sunrise ; watch the light Leap from his chariot on the loftiest peak, And thence descend triumphant, step by step, The stairway of the hills. Free air and action Will soon dispel these vapours of the brain. Julian. My friend, if one should tell a homeless boy,

" There is your father's house : go in and rest; " Through every open room the child would go, Timidly looking for the friendly eye ; Fearing to touch, scarce daring even to wonder At what he saw, until he found his sire.

But gathered to his bosom, straight he is The heir of all; he knows it 'midst his tears. And so with me : not having seen Him yet, The light rests on me with a heaviness j All beauty wears to me a doubtful look ; A voice is in the wind I do not know ; A meaning on the face of the high hills Whose utterance I cannot comprehend. A something is behind them : that is God. These are his words, I doubt not, language
strange ;

These are the expressions of his shining thoughts , And he is present, but I find him not. I have not yet been held close to his heart. Once in his inner room, and by his eyes Acknowledged, I shall find my home in these, ? Mid sights familiar as a mother's smiles, And sounds that never lose love's mystery. Then they will comfort me. Lead me to Him

Robert (pointing to the Crucifix in a recess). See,
there is God revealed in human form ! Julian (kneeling and crossing], Alas, my friend !

—revealed—but as in nature : I see the man ; I cannot find the God. I know his voice is in the wind, his presence Is in the Christ. The wind blows where it listeth j And there stands Manhood : and the God is there, Not here, not here.

[Pointing to us bosom. Seeing Robert's bewildered look, and changing his tone.

You understand me not. Without my need, you cannot know my want. You will all night be puzzling to determine With which of the old heretics to class me. But you are honest; will not rouse the cry Against me. I am honest. For the proof, Such as will satisfy a monk, look here ! Is this a smooth belt, brother ? And look here !

Did one week's scourging seam my side like that ? I am ashamed to speak thus, and to show Things rightly hidden; but in my heart I love you, And cannot bear but you should think me true. Let it excuse my foolishness. They talk Of penance ! Let them talk when they have tried, And found it has not even unbarred heaven's gate, Let out one stray beam of its living light, Or humbled that proud that knows not God. You are my friend :—if you should find this cell Empty some morning, do not be afraid That any ill has happened.

Robert. Well, perhaps
'Twere better you should go. I cannot help you, But I can keep your secret. God be with you. [Goes.

Julian. Amen.—A good man; but he has
not waked,

And seen the Sphinx's stony eyes fixed on him. God veils it. He believes in Christ, he thinks ; VOL. i. c

And so he does, as possible for him.
How he will wonder when he looks -for heaven !
He thinks me an enthusiast, because
I seek to know God, and to hear his voice
Talk to my heart in silence ; as of old
The Hebrew king, when, still, upon his bed,
He lay communing with his heart; and God
With strength in his soul did strengthen him, until
In His light he saw light. God speaks to men.
My soul leans towards him ; stretches forth its
arms,

And waits expectant. Speak to me, my God ; And let me know the living Father cares For me, even me ; for this one of his children. — Hast thou no word for me ? I am thy thought. God, let thy mighty heart beat into mine, And let mine answer as a pulse to thine. See, I am low ; yea, very low ; but thou Art high, and thou canst lift me up to thee.

SCENE n. WITHIN AND WITHOUT.
I am a child, a fool before thee, God ;
But thou hast made my weakness as my strength.
I am an emptiness for thee to fill;
My soul, a cavern for thy sea. I lie
Diffused, abandoning myself to thee
1 will look up, if life should fail in
looking.

Ah me ! A stream cut from my parent-spring! Ah me ! A life lost from its father-life !

SCENE II.— The refectory. The monks at table. A buzz of conversation. ROBERT enters, 'wiping his forehead, as if he had just come in.

Stephen (speaking across the table]. You see, my

friend, it will not stand to logic; Or, if you like it better, stand to reason ; For in this doctrine is involved a cause Which for its very being doth depend Upon its own effect. For, don't you see,

ca

He tells me to have faith and I shall live ?
Have faith for what ? Why, plainly, that I shall
Be saved from hell by him, and ta'en to heaven;
What is salvation else ? If I believe,
Then he will save me. . . But this his will
Has no existence till that I believe ;
So there is nothing for my faith to rest on,
No object for belief. How can I trust
In that which is not ? Send the salad, Cosmo.
Besides, 'twould be a plenary indulgence ;
To all intents save one, most plenary—
And that the Church's coffer. 'Tis absurd.
Monk. 'Tis most absurd, as you have clearly

shown.

And yet I fear some of us have been nibbling At this same heresy. 'Twere well that one Should find it poison. I have no pique at him — But there's that Julian —

Stephen. Hush ! speak lower, friend.

Two blotiksfurt/ier down tfie table — in a tow tone.

1st Monk. Where did you find her ?

2nd Monk. She was taken ill

At the Star-in-the-East. I chanced to pass that

way,

And so they called me in. I found her dying. But ere she would confess and make her peace, She begged to know if I had ever seen About this neighbourhood, a tall dark man, Moody and silent, with a little stoop As if his eyes were heavy for his shoulders, And a strange look of mingled youth and age,—

1st Moid'. Julian, by

2nd Monk. 'St—no names ! I had not seen

him.

I saw the death-mist gathering in her eye, And urged her to proceed; and she began ; But went not far before delirium came, With endless repetitions, hurryings forward,

Recovering like a hound at fault The past

Was running riot in her conquered brain ;

And there, with doors thrown wide, a motley

group

Held carnival; went freely out and in, Meeting and jostling. But withal it seemed As some confused tragedy went on ; Till suddenly the lights sunk out; the pageant Went like a ghost; the chambers of her brain Lay desolate and silent. I can gather This much, and nothing more. This Julian Is one of some distinction ; probably rich, And titled Count. He had a love-affair, In good-boy, layman fashion, seemingly. Give me the woman; love is troublesome. She loved him too, but false play came between, And used this woman for her minister ; Who never would have peached, but for a witness Hidden behind some curtains in her heart

Of which she did not know. That same, her conscience,

Has waked and blabbed so far; but must conclude Its story to some double-ghostly father, For she is ghostly penitent by this. Our consciences will play us no such tricks ; They are the Church's, not our own. We must Keep this small matter secret. If it should Come to his ears, he'll soon bid us good-bye — A lady's love before ten heavenly crowns ! And so the world will have the benefit Of the said wealth of his, if such there be. I have told you, old Godfrey; I tell none else Until our Abbot comes.

1st Monk. That is to-morrow.

Another group near the bottom oftfte table, in which is ROBERT.

1st Monk. 'Tis very clear there's something wrong with him.

Have you not marked that look, half scorn, half

pity,

Which passes like a thought across his face, When he has listened, seeming scarce to listen, A while to our discourse ?—he never joins.

2nd Monk. I know quite well. I stood beside

him once,

Some of the brethren near ; Stephen was talking. He chanced to say the words, Otir Holy

Faith. " Faith indeed ! poor fools ! " fell from his lips, Half-muttered, and half-whispered, as the words Had wandered forth unbidden. I am sure He is an atheist at the least.

•$rd Monk (pale-faced and large-eyed\'7d. And I Fear he is something worse. I had a trance In which the devil tempted me : the shape Was Julian's to the very finger-nails. Non nobis, Domine ! I overcame. I am sure of one thing—music tortures him :

I saw him once, amidst the Gloria Patri, When the whole chapel trembled in the sound, Rise slowly as in ecstasy of pain, Arid stretch his arms abroad, and clasp his hands. Then slowly, faintingly, sink on his knees.

2nd Monk. He does not knojv his rubric;

stands when others

Are kneeling round him. I have seen him twice With his missal upside down.

47 Monk (plethoric and husky?). He blew his

nose Quite loud on last Annunciation-day,

I And choked our Lady's name in the Abbot's throat. Robert. When he returns, we must complain j and beg He'll take such measures as the case requires.

SCENE III.— Julian's cell. An o£en chest. The lantern on a stool, its candle nearly burnt out. JULIAN lying on his bed, looking at the light.

Julian. And so all growth that is not towards

God

Is growing to decay. All increase gained Is but an ugly, earthy, fungous growth. 'Tis aspiration as that wick aspires, Towering above the light it overcomes, But ever sinking with the dying flame.

0 let me live, if but a daisy's life !

No toadstool life-in-death, no efflorescence ! Wherefore wilt thou not hear me, Lord of me ? Have I no claim on thee? Tine, I have none That springs from me, but much that springs from

thee. Hast thou not made me ? Liv'st thou not in me ?

1 have done nought for thee, am but a want;

But thou who art rich in giving, canst give claims; And this same need of thee, which thou hast given, Is a strong claim on thee to give thyself, And makes me bold to rise and come to thee. Through all my sinning thou hast not recalled This witness of thy fatherhood, to plead For thee with me, and for thy child with thee. Last night, as now, I seemed to speak with

Him;

Or was it but my heart that spoke for him ? "Thou mak'st me long," I said, " therefore wilt give;

My longing is thy promise, O my God. If, having sinned, I thus have lost the claim, Why doth the longing yet remain with me, And make me bold thus to besiege thy doors ? " I thought I heard an answer: " Question on. Keep on thy need; it is the bond that holds Thy being yet to mine. I give it thee,

A hungering and a fainting and a pain, Yet a God-blessing. Thou art not quite dead While this pain lives in thee. I bless thee with it. Better to live in pain than die that death."

So I will live, and nourish this my pain; For oft it giveth birth unto a hope That makes me strong in prayer. He knows it

loo.

Softly I'll walk the earth; for it is his, Not mine to revel in. Content I wait. A still small voice 1 cannot but believe, Says on within : God will reveal himself.

I must go from this place. I cannot rest. It boots not staying. A desire like thirst Awakes within me, or a new child-heart, To be abroad on the mysterious earth, Out with the moon in all the blowing winds.

'Tis strange that dreams of her should come again.

For many months I had not seen her form, Save phantom-like on dim hills of the past, Until I laid me down an hour ago ; When twice through the dark chamber, full of

eyes,

The dreamful fact passed orderly and true. Once more I see the house ; the inwai'd blaze Of the glad windows half-quenched in the moon ; The trees that, drooping, murmured to the wind, " Ah ! wake me not," which left them to their

sleep,

All save the poplar : it was full of joy, So that it could not sleep, but trembled on. Sudden as Aphrodite from the sea, She issued radiant from the pearly night. It took me half with fear— the glimmer and gleam Of her white festal garments, haloed round With denser moonbeams. On she came—and there I am bewildered. Something I remember

Of thoughts that choked the passages of sound,

Hurrying forth without their pilot-words ;

Of agony, as when a spirit seeks

In vain to hold communion with a man ;

A hand that would and would not stay in mine;

A gleaming of her garments far away;

And then I know not what. The moon was

low, When from the earth I rose; my hair was wet,

Dripping with dew—

Enter ROBERT caittiously.

Why, how now, Robert ? [Rising- on his elbow.

Robert (glancing at the chest\'7d. I see; that's well.

Are you nearly ready ? Julian. Why? What's the matter? Robert. You must go this night, If you would go at all.

Julian. Why must I go ?

Robert (turning over the things in the chest\'7d. TIere, put this coat on. Ah! take that thing too. No more such head-gear ! Have you not a hat,

[Going to the chest again.

Or something for your head? There's such a

hubbub

Got up about you ! The Abbot comes to-morrow. Julian. Ah, well! I need not ask. I know it

all. Robert. No, you do not. Nor is there time to

tell you.

Ten minutes more, they will be round to bar The outer doors ; and then—good-bye, poor Julian!

JULIAN is rapidly changing his clothes. Julian. Now I am ready, Robert. Thank you, friend. Farewell ! God bless you ! We shall meet again.

Robert. Farewell, dear friend ! Keep far away from this. [Goes.

JULIAN follows htm out of the cell, steps along a narrow passage to a door, which he opens slowly. He goes out, and closes the door be' hind him.

SCENE IV.— Night. The court of a country-inn. The ABBOT, while his horse is brought out.

Abbot. Now for a shrine to house this rich
Madonna,
Within the holiest of the holy place ! I'll have it made in fashion as a stable, With porphyry pillars to a marble stall; And odorous woods, shaved fine like shaken hay, Shall fill the silver manger for a bed, Whereon shall lie the ivory Infant carved By shepherd hands on plains of Bethlehem. And over him shall bend the Mother mild, In silken white, and coroneted gems.

Glorious ! But wherewithal I see not now—
The Mammon of unrighteousness is scant;
Nor know I any nests of money-bees
That would yield half-contentment to my need.
Yet will I trust and hope ; for never yet
In journeying through this vale of tears have I
Projected pomp that did not blaze anon.

SCENE V.— After midnight. JULIAN seated wider a tree on the roadside.

Julian. So lies my journey—on into the dark. Without my will I find myself alive, And must go forward. Is it God that draws Magnetic all the souls unto their home, Travelling, they know not how, but unto God ? It matters little what may come to me Of outward circumstance, as hunger, thirst, Social condition, yea, or love or hate ; But what shall be, fifty summers hence ?

VOL I. D

My life, my being, all that meaneth me, Goes darkling forward into something—what ?
0 God, thou knowest. It is not my care.
If thou wert less than truth, or less than love,
It were a fearful thing to be and grow
We know not what. My God, take care of me
Pardon and swathe me in an infinite love
Pervading and inspiring me, thy child.
And let thy own design in me work on,
Unfolding the ideal man in me !
Which being greater far than I have grown,
1 cannot comprehend. I am thine, not mine. One day, completed unto thine intent,
I shall be able to discourse with thee ;
For thy Idea, gifted with a self,
Must be of one with the mind where it sprang,
And fit to talk with thee about thy thoughts.
Lead me, O Father, holding by thy hand ;
I a*k not whither, for it must be on.
This road will lead me to the hills, I think ; And there I am in safety and at home.

SCENE VI.— The A bboCs room. The Abbot and one of the Monks.

Abbot. Did she say Julian ? Did she say the
name ?
. Monk. She did.
Abbot. What did she call the lady ? What ? Monk. I could not hear. Abbot. Nor where she lived \
Monk. Nor that.

She was too wild for leading where I would. Abbot. So. Send Julian. One thing I need not
ask :

You have kept this matter secret ? Monk. Yes, my lord.

Abbot. Well, go, and send him hither.

[Monk goes.

Said I well, bi

That wish would burgeon into pomp for me ? That God will hear his own elect who cry ?
Now for a shrine, so glowing in the means That it shall draw the eyes by power of light 1 So
tender in conceit, that it shall diaw The heart by very strength of delicateness, And move proud
thought to worship !

I must act

With caution now ; must win his confidence ; •Question him of the secret enemies That
fight against his soul; and lead him thus 'To tell me, by degrees, his history. So shall I find the
truth, and lay foundation ^For future acts, as circumstance requires. dFor if the tale be true that
he is rich, And

Re-enter Monk in haste and terror. Monk. He's gone, my lord J His cell is empty.

Abbot (starting up\'7d. What! You are crazy!

Gone ! His cell is empty ! Monk. 'Tis true as death, my lord. Abbot. Heaven and hell! It
shall not be, I

swear !

There is a plot in this ! You, sir, have lied ! Some one is in his confidence—who is it ?
Go rouse the convent. [Monk^»«.

He must be followed, found. Hunt's up, friend Julian ! First your heels, old

stag!

But by and by your horns, and then your side ! 'Tis venison much too good for the world's
eating.

I'll go and sift this business to the bran. Robert and him I have sometimes seen together.
God's curse ! it shall fare ill with any man That has connived at this, if I detect him.

SCENE VII,— Afternoon. The mountains. JULIAN.

Julian. Once more I tread thy courts, O God

of heaven!

I lay my hand upon a rock, whose peak Is miles away, and high amidst the clouds.
Perchance I touch the mountain whose blue

summit,

With the fantastic rock upon its side, Stops the eye's flight from that high chamber-
window

Where, when a boy, I used to sit and gaze With wondering awe upon the mighty thing,
Terribly calm, alone, self-satisfied, The hitherto of my child thoughts. Beyond, A sea might roar
around its base. Beyond, Might be the depths of the unfathomed space, This the earth's bulwark
over the abyss. Upon its very point I have watched a star

For a few moments ciown it with a fire, As of an incense-offering that blazed Upon this
mighty altar high uplift, And then float up the pathless waste of heaven. From the next window I
could look abroad Over a plain unrolled, which God had painted With trees, and meadow-grass,
and a large river, Where boats went to and fro like water-flies, In white and green ; but still I
turned to look At that one mount, aspiring o'er its fellows : All here I saw—I knew not what was
there.

0 love of knowledge and of mystery, Striving together in the heart of man !

"Tell me, and let me know; explain the thing."— Then when the courier-thoughts have circled round: "Alas ! I know it all; its charm is gone ! " But I must hasten ; else the sun will set Before I reach the smoother valley-road.

1 wonder if my old nurse lives ; or has

Eyes left to know me with. Surely, I think, Four years of wandering since I left my home, In sunshine and in snow, in ship and cell, Must have worn changes in this face of mine Sufficient to conceal me, if I will.

SCENE VIII.— A dungeon in the monastery. A ray of the moon on the floor. ROBERT.

Robert. One comfort is, he's far away by this. Perhaps this comfort is my deepest sin. Where shall I find a daysman in this strife Between my heart and holy Church's words ? Is not the law of kindness from God's finger, Yea, from his heart, on mine ? But then we must Deny ourselves ; and impulses must yield, Be subject to the written law of words ; Impulses made, made strong, that we might have Within the temple's court live things to bring And slay upon his altar ; that we may,

By this hard penance of the heart and soul, Become the slaves of Christ. — I have done wrong; I ought not to have let poor Julian go. And yet that light upon the floor says, yes— Christ would have let him go. It seemed a good, Yes, self-denying deed, to risk my life That he might be in peace. Still up and down The balance goes, a good in either scale ; Two angels giving each to each the lie, And none to part them or decide the question. But still the words come down the heaviest Upon my conscience as that scale descends ; But that may be because they hurt me more, Being rough strangers in the feelings' home. Would God forbid us to do what is right, Even for his sake ? But then Julian's life Belonged to God, to do with as he pleases. I am bewildered. 'Tis as God and God Commanded different things in different tones.

Ah! then, the tones are different: which is likest God's voice ? The one is gentle, loving, kind, Like Mary singing to her mangered child ; The other like a self-restrained tempest; Like— ah, alas !—the trumpet on Mount Sinai, Louder and louder, and the voice of words.

0 for some light! Would they would kill me

then

would go up, close up, to God's own throne, And ask, and beg, and pray, to know the truth ; And he would slay this ghastly contradiction.

T should not fear, for he would comfort me, Because I am perplexed, and long to know. But this perplexity may be my sin, And come of pride that will not yield to him. O for one word from God ! his own, and fresh From him to me ! Alas ! what shall I do ?

END OF PART I.

WITHIN AND WITHOUT.

PART II.

HARK, hark, a voice amid the quiet intense ! It is thy Duty waiting thee without. Rise from thy knees in hope, the half of doubt; A hand doth pull thee—it is Providence ; Open thy door straightway, and get thee* hence ; Go forth into the tumult and the shout ; Work, love, with workers, lovers, all about : Of noise alone is born the inward sense Of silence ; and from action springs alone The inward knowledge of true love and faith. Then, weary, go thou back with failing breath, And in thy chamber make thy prayer and moan : One day upon His bosom, all thine own, Thou shalt lie still, embraced in holy death.

PART II.

SCENE I.— A room in Julians castle, JULIAN and tht

old Nurse.

Julian. Nembroni ? Count Nembroni ?—I remember :

A man about my height, but stronger built ? I have seen him at her father's. There was something

I did not like about him. — Ah ! I know : He had a way of darting looks at one, As if he wished to know you, but by stealth.

Nurse. The same, my lord. He is the creditor. The common story is, he sought his daughter, But sought in vain : the lady would not wed.

'Twas rumoured soon they were in grievous trouble, Which caused much wonder, for the family Was always counted wealthy. Count Nembroni

Contrived to be the only creditor,

And so imprisoned him.

Julian. Where is the lady ?

Nurse. Down in the town.

Julian. But where ?

Nurse. If you turn left,

When you go through the gate, 'tis the last house Upon this side the way. An honest couple, Who once were almost pensioners of hers, Have given her shelter, till she find a home With distant friends. Alas, poor lady ! 'tis A wretched change for her.

Julian. Hm ! ah ! I see.

What kind of man is this Nembroni, nurse ?

Nurse. Here he is little known. His title comes From an estate, they say, beyond the hills.

He looks ungracious : I have seen the children Run to the doors when he came up the street.

Julian. Thank you, nurse; you may go. Stay

—one thing more. Have any of my people seen me ?

Nurse, None

But me, my lord.

Jtdian. And can you keep it secret ?- -

I know you will for my sake. I will trust you. Bring me some supper ; I am tired and faint. [Nurse goes.

Poor and alone ! Such a man has not laid Such plans for nothing further. I will watch him. Heaven may have brought me hither for her sake. Poor child ! I would protect thee as thy father, Who cannot help thee. Thou wast not to blame, My love had no claim on like love from thee.— How the old love comes gushing to my heart!

I know not what I can do yet but watch,

I have no hold on him. I cannot go,

Say, I suspect: and, Is it so or not?

I should but injure them by doing so.

True, I might pay her father's debts ; and will,

If Joseph, my old friend, has managed well

During my absence. have not spent much.

But still she'd be in danger from this man,

If not permitted to betray himself;

And I, discovered, could no more protect.

Or if, unseen by her, I yet could haunt

Her footsteps like an angel, not for long
Should I remain unseen of other eyes,
That peer from under cowls—not angel-eyes—
Hunting me out, over the stormy earth.
No; I must watch. I can do nothing better.

SCENE II.— A poor cottage. An old Man and Woman sitting together.

Man, How's the poor lady now ?

Woman. She's poorly still.
I fancy every day she's growing thinner. I am sure she's wasting steadily.

Man. Has the count
Been here again to-day ?

Woman. No. And I think
He will not come again. She was so proud The last time he was here, you would have thought She was a queen at least.

Man. Remember, wife,
What she has been. Trouble and that throws down The common folk like us all of a heap : With folks like her, that are high bred and blood, It sets the mettle up.

Woman. All very right;
But take her as she was, she might do worse Than wed the Count Nenibroni.

Man. Possible.
But are you sure there is no other man
VOL. I.
Stands in his way ?

Woman. How can I tell ? So be,
He should be here to help her. What she'll do I am sure I do not know. We cannot keep her.
A.nd for her work, she does it far too well fo earn a living by it. Her times are changed— She should not give herself such prideful airs. Man. Come, come, old wife ! you women are so hard
On one another ! You speak fair for men, And make allowances ; but when a woman Crosses your way, you speak the worst of her. But where is this you're going then to-night ? Do they want me to go as well as you ?

Woman. Yes, you must go, or else it is no use.
They cannot give the money to me, except My husband go with me. He told me so.

Man. Well, wife, it's worth the going—just to see: I don't expect a groat to come of it.

SCENE III.—Kitchen of a small inn. Host and Hostess.

Host. That's a queer customer you've got up stairs; What the deuce is he ?

Hostess. What is that to us ?
He always pays his way, and handsomely. I wish there were more like him.

Host. Has he been
At home all day ?

Hostess. He has not stirred a foot
Across the threshold. That's his only fault — He's always in the way.

Host. What does he do ?

Hostess. Paces about the room, or sits at the window.

B 2

S* WITHIN AND WITHOUT. PART a.

I sometimes make an errand to the cupboard, To see what he's about : he looks annoyed, But does not speak a word.

Host. He must be crazed,

Or else in hiding for some scrape or other. Hostess. He has a wild look in his eye some-times j

But sure he would not sit so much in the dark, If he were mad, or anything on his conscience ; And though he does not say much, when he

speaks A civiller man ne'er came in woman's way.

Host. Oh ! he's all right, I warrant. Is the wine come ?

SCENE IV.— The inn', a room upstairs. JULIAN at the window, half hidden by the curtain.

Julian. With what profusion Ij^r white fingers spend

Delicate motions on the insensate cloth ! It was so late this morning ere she came ! I fear she has been ill. She looks so pak! Her beauty is much less, but she more lovely. Do I not love her more than when that beauty Beamed out like starlight, radiating beyond The confines of her wondrous face and form, And animated with a present power The outmost folds and waves of drapery ?

Ha ! there is something now : the old woman

drest

In her Sunday clothes, and waiting at the door, As for her husband. Something will follow this. And here he comes, all in his best like her. They will be gone a while. Slowly they walk, With short steps down the street Now I must

wake The sleeping hunter-eagle in my eyes !

SCENE V.— A back street. Two Servants with a carriage and pair.

1st, Serv. Heavens, what a cloud! as big as

^Etna! There !

That gust blew stormy. Take Juno by the head, I'll stand by Neptune. Take her head, I say ; We'll have enough to do, if it should lighten.

2nd Serv. Such drops ! That's the first of it.

I declare

She spreads her nostrils and looks wild already, As if she smelt it coming. I wish we were Under some roof or other. I fear this business Is not of the right sort.

1st. Serv. He looked as black

As if he too had lightning in his bosom. There ! Down, you brute ! Mind the pole, Beppo

1

SCENE VI.— Ziau's room. JULIAN standing at the •window, his face pressed against a Pane. Storm and gathering darkness without.

"Julian. Plague on the lamp ! 'tis gone—no,

there it flares !

I wish the wind would leave or blow it out. Heavens ! how it thunders ! This terrific storm Will either cow or harden him. I'm blind ! That lightning ! Oh, let me see again, lest he Should enter in the dark ! I cannot bear This glimmering longer. Now that gusli of rain Has blotted all my view with crossing lights. 'Tis no use waiting here. I must cross over, And take my stand in the corner by the door. But if he comes while I go down the stairs, And I not see ? To make sure, I'll go gently Up the stair to the landing by her door.

\He goes quickly towards the door.

Hostess (opening the door and looking in\'7d. If you please, Sir— [He hurries past.

The devil's in the man !

SCENE Vll.—The landing.

Voice "within. If you scream, I must muffle you. Julian (rushing up the stair). He is there !

His hand is on her mouth ! She tries to scream !

[Flinging the door open, as NEMBRONI springs forward on the other side.

Back! Nembroni. What the devil!—Beggar !

[Drawing his sword, and making a thrust at JULIAN, which he parries with his left arm, as, drawing his dagger, he springs within NEMBKONI'S guard.

Julian (taking him by the throat). I have faced worse storms than you. [They struggle.

Heart point and hilt strung on the line of force,

[Stalling him.

SCENE vii. WITHIN AND WITHOUT. y,

Your ribs will not mail your heart !

[NEMBRONi. dead. JULIAN wipes his dagget on the dead man's coat.

If men will be devils,

They are better in hell than here.

\Lightningflashes on the blade. What a night For a soul to go out of doors ! God in Heaven !

[Approaching the lady within.

Ah ! she has fainted. That is well. I hope

It will not pass too soon. It is not far

To the half-hidden door in my own fence,

And that is well. If I step carefully,

Such rain will soon wash out the tell-tale foot-prints.

What! blood! He does not bleed much, I should

think.

Oh, I see ! it is mine—he has wounded me. That's awkward now.

[Taking a handkerchief from the floor by the window*

Pardon me, dear lady ;

[.Tying the handkerchief with hand and teeth round his arm.

'Tis not to save my blood I would defile

Even your handkerchief.

[Coming towards the door, carrying her.

I am pleased to think Ten monkish months have not ta'en all my

strength.

[Looking out of the wind<nv on the landing.

For once, thank darkness ! 'Twas sent for us, not him. [He goes down the stair.

SCENE VIII. A room in the castle. JULIAN and the Nurse.

Julian. Ask me no questions now, my dear old

nurse.

You have put your charge to bed ? Nurse. Yes, my dear lord.

Julian, And has she spoken yet ?

Nurse. After you left,

Her eyelids half unclosed j she murmured once : Where am /, mother ? —then she looked at me, And her eyes wandered over all my face; Till half in comfort, half in weariness, They closed again. Bless her, dear soul! she is As feeble as a child.

Julian. Under your care,

She will recover soon. Let no one know She is in the house:—blood has been shed for her.

Nurse. Alas ! I feared it ; for her dress is bloody.

Julian. That's mine, not his. But put it in the

fire. Get her another. I'll leave a purse with you.

Nurse. Leave ?

Julian. Yes. I am off to-night, wan*

dering again Over the earth and sea. She must not know

I have been here. You must contrive to keep My share a secret. Once she moved and spoke When a branch caught her; but she could not see me. She thought, no doubt, it was Nembroni had her. Nor would she have known me. You must hide

her, nurse.

Let her on no pretence know where she is, Nor utter word that might awake a guess. When she is well and wishes to be gone, Then write to this address—but under cover

\Writing.

To the Prince Calboli at Florence. I Will manage all the rest. But let her know Her father is set free ; assuredly, Ere you can give the news, it will be so. Nurse. How shall I best conceal her, my good

lord?

Julian, I have thought of that. There's a deserted room

SCENE vin. WITHIN AND WITHOUT. 61

In the old south wing, at the further end Of the oak gallery.

Ntirse. Not deserted quite.

I ventured, when you left, to make it mine, Because you loved it when a boy, my lord.

jTilian. You do not know, nurse, why I loved

it though :

I found a sliding panel, and a door Into a room behind. I'll show it you. You'll find some musty traces of me yet, When you go in. Now take her to your room,

ut get the other ready. Light a fire, And keep it burning well for several days. Then, one by one, out of the other rooms, Take everything to make it comfortable; Quietly, you know. If you must have your

daughter,

Bind her to be as secret as yourself. Then put her there. I'll let her father know

She is in safety.—I must change my clothes, And be far off or ever morning breaks.

[Nurse goes.

My treasure-room ! how little then I thought, Glad in my secret, one day it would hold A treasure unto which I dared not come. Perhaps she'd love me now—a very little ?— But not with even a heavenly gift would I Go beg her love j that should be free as light, Cleaving unto myself even for myself. I have enough to brood on, joy to turn Over and over in my secret heart:— She lives, and is the better that I live.

Re-enter Nurse. Nurse. My lord, her mind is wandering ; she
is raving;
She's in a dreadful fever. We must send To Arli for the doctor, else her life Will be in
danger.

Julian (rising disturbed]. Go and fetch your
daughter.
Take her at once to your own room, and there I'll see her. Can you manage it between
you ? Nurse. O yes, my lord; she is so thin, poor child ! [Nurse goes.

Julian. I ought to know the way to treat a
fever,
If it be one of twenty. Hers has come Of low food, wasting, and anxiety. I've seen enough
of that in Prague and Smyrna.

SCENE IX.— The Abbofs room in the monastery. The Abbot.

Abbot. 'Tis useless all. No trace of him found
yet. One hope remains : we'll see what Stephen says.

Enter STEPHEN. Stephen, I have sent for you, because I am told
You said to-day, if I commissioned you, You'd scent him out, if skulking in his grave,
Stephen. I did, my lord.

Abbot. How would you do it,
Stephen ?
Stephen. Try one plan till it failed; then try
another;
Try half-a-dozen plans at once; keep eyes And ears wide open, and mouth shut, my lord j
Your bull-dog sometimes makes the best retriever, I have no plan ; but, give me time and money,
I'll find him out.

Abbot. Stephen, you're just the man
I have been longing for. Get yourself ready.

SCENE X.— Towards morning. The Nurse's room. LILIA in led. JULIAN -watching.

Julian. I think she sleeps. Would God it were so; then
She would do well. What strange things she has
spoken !
My heart is beating as if it would spend Its life in this one night, and beat it out. No
wonder ! there is more of life's delight In one hour such as this than many years ; For life is
measured by intensity, Not by the how much of the crawling clock.

Is that a bar of moonlight stretched across The window-blind ? or is it but a band Of
whiter cloth my thrifty dame has sewed Upon the other ?—No ; it is the moon Low down in the
west. 'Twas such a moon as this—

Litia (half-asleep, wildly]. If Julian had been
here, you dared not do it — Julian ! Julian ! [.Half rising.

Julian (forgetting his caution, and going up to
her\'7d. I am here, my Lilia. No. VOL. r. F
Put your head down, my love. 'Twas all a dream,
A terrible dream. Gone now—is it not ?
[She looks at him with wide restless eyes; then sinks back on the pillow. He leaves her.
How her dear eyes bewildered looked at me ! But her soul's eyes are closed. If this last

long She'll die before my sight, and Joy will lead In by the hand her sister, Grief, pale-faced, And leave her to console my solitude. Ah, what a joy ! I dare not think of it! And what a grief! I will not think of that! Love ? and from her ? my beautiful, my own ! O God, I did not know thou wert so rich In making and in giving. I knew not The gathered glory of this earth of thine. Oh ! wilt thou crush me with an infinite joy ? Make me a god by giving—making mine Thy centre-thought of living beauty ?—sprung

From thee, and coming home to dwell with me !

[He leans on the wall.

Lilia (softly). Am I in heaven ? There's something makes me glad, As if I were in heaven ! Yes, yes, I am. I see the flashing of ten thousand glories ; I hear the trembling of a thousand wings, That vibrate music on the murmuring air ! Each tiny feather-blade crushes its pool Of circling air to sound, and quivers music. — What is it, though, that makes me glad like this ? I knew, but cannot find it — I forget. It must be here   what was it ?—Hark ! the fall, The endless going of the stream of life!— Ah me ! I thirst, I thirst,—I am so thirsty !

[Querulously.

QULIAN gives her drink, supporting her. She looks at hint again, with, large -wondering eyes.

Ah ! now I know—I was so very thirsty !

[He lays her down. Site is comforted, and falls asleep. He extinguishes the light, and looks out of the "window.

F 3

Julian. The grey earth dawning up, cold, comfortless ;

With an obtrusive I am written large Upon its face !

[Approaching the bed, and gazing on LILIA silently with clasfed hands; then returning to the window.

She sleeps so peacefully !

0 God, I thank thee : thou hast sent her sleep. Lord, let it sink into her heart and brain.

Enter Nurse.

Oh, nurse, I'm glad you're come. She is asleep. You must be near her when she wakes again.

1 think she'll be herself. But do be careful— Right cautious how you tell her I am here.

Sweet woman-child, may God be in your sleep !

[JULIAN goes.

Nurse. Bless her white face ! She looks just like my daughter,

That's now a saint in heaven. Just those thin

cheeks,

And eyelids hardly closed over her eyes ! Go on, poor darling ! you are drinking life From the breast of sleep. And yet I fain would see Your shutters open, for I then should know Whether the soul had drawn her curtains back, To peep at morning from her own bright windows. Ah, what a joy is ready, waiting her, To break her fast upon, if her wild dreams Have but betrayed her secrets honestly ! Will he not give thee love as dear as thine ?

SCENE XL— A hilly road. STEPHEN, trudging alone, pauses to look around him.

Stephen. Not a footprint! not a trace that a bloodhound would nose at! But Stephen shall be acknowledged a good dog and true. If I had him within stick-length — mind thy head, brother Julian ! Thou hast not hair enough to protect it, and thy tonsure shall not. Neither shalt thou tarry at Jericho.—It is a poor man that leaves no trail ; and if thou wert poor, I would not follow thee.

Sings.

Oh ! many a hound is stretching out

His two legs or his four, Where the saddled horses stand about

The court and the castle door; Till out comes the baron, jolly and stout,

To hunt the bristly boar.

The emperor, he doth keep a pack

In his antechambers standing, And up and down the stairs, good lack I

And eke upon the landing : A straining leash, and a quivering back,

And nostrils and chest expanding !

The devil a hunter long has been,

Though Doctor Luther said it: Of his canon-pack he was the dean,

And merrily he led it: To fatten them up, when game is lean

He keeps his dogs on credit

Each man is a hunter to his trade,

And they follow one another ; But such a hunter never was made

As the monk that hunted his brother ! And the runaway pig, alive or dead,

Shall be eaten by its mother.

Better hunt a flea in a woolly blanket, than a leg-bail monk in this wilderness of mountains, forests, and precipices ! But the flea may be caught, and so shall the monk. I have said it. He is well spotted, with his silver crown, and his uncropped ears. The rascally vow-breaker ! But his vows shall keep him, whether he keep them or not. The whining, blubbering idiot! Gave his plaything, and wants it back !—I wonder whereabouts I am.

SCENE XII.— The Nurse s room. LILIA sitting njt> in bed. JULIAN seated by her', an oj>en note in his hand.

Lilia. Tear it up, Julian.

Julian. No ; I'll treasure it

As the remembrance of a by-gone grief: I love it well, because it is not yours. Lilia. Where have you been these long, long

years away ? You look much older. You have suffered,

Julian ! Julian. Since that day, Lilia, I have seen much,

thought much ;

Suffered perhaps a little. But of this We'll say no more. When you are quite yourself, I'll tell you all you want to know about me. Lilia. Do tell me something now. I feel quite strong; It will not hurt me.

Julian. Wait a day or two.

Indeed 'twould weary you to tell you all.

Lilia. And I have much to tell you, Juliaa I

Have suffered too — not all for my own sake.

\'7bRecalling something.

Oh, what a dream I had ! Oh, Julian !— I don't know when it was. It must have been Before you brought me here : I am sure it was. Julian. Don't speak about it. Tell me afterwards.

You must keep quiet now. Indeed you must. Lilia. I will obey you, and not speak a word.

Enter Nurse. Nurse. Blessings upon her! she's near well

already.

Who would have thought, three days ago, to see You look so bright? My lord, you have

done
wonders.

Julian. 'Tis not my work, dame.—I must leave you now.
To please me, Lilia, go to sleep awhile.

[JULIAN goes.

Lilia. Why does he always wear that curious
cap?

Nurse. I don't know. You must sleep. Lilia. Yes. I forgot.

SCENE XIII.— The Steward's room. JULIAN and the Steward. Papers on tJif table,
•which JULIAN has just finished examining.

Julian. Thank you much, Joseph; you have
done well for me. You sent that note privately to my friend ?

Steward. I did, my lord; and have conveyed
the money,

l'utting all things in train for his release, Without appearing in it personally, Or giving
any clue to other hands. He sent this message by my messenger : His hearty thanks, and God will
bless you for it. He will be secret. For his daughter, she
Is safe with you as with himself; and so God bless you both ! He will expect to hear From
both of you from England.

Julian. Well, again.
What money is remaining in your hands ?

Steward. Two bags, three hundred each ; that's
all. I fear To wake suspicion, if I call in more.

Julian. Quite right. One thing besides : lest a
mischance

Befall us, though I do not fear it much— We have been very secret—is that boat I had
before I left, in sailing trim ?

Steward. I knew it was a favourite with my
lord;

I've taken care of it. A month ago With my own hands I painted it all fresh, Fitting new
oars and rowlocks. The old sail I'll have replaced immediately ; and then
'Twill be as good as new.

Julian. That's excellent.
Well, launch it in the evening. Make it fast To the stone steps behind my garden study.
Stow in the lockers some sea-stores, and put The money in the old desk in the study.

Steward. I will, my lord. It will be safe enough.

SCENE XIV.— A road near the town. A Waggoner. STEPHEN, in lay dress, coming up
to him.

Stephen. Whose castle's that upon the hill, good fellow ?

Waggoner. Its present owner's of the Uglii; They call him Lorenzino,

Stephen. Whose is that
Down in the valley ?

Waggoner. That is Count Lamballa's.

Stephen. What is his Christian name ?

Waggoner. Omfredo. No,
That was his father's ; his is Julian.

Stephen. Is he at home ?

Waggoner. No, not for many a day.

His steward, honest man, I know is doubtful Whether he be alive ; and yet his land Is better farmed than any in the country.

Stephen. He is not married, then ?

Waggoner. No. There's a gossip

Amongst the women—but who would heed their

talking ? — That love half-crazed, then drove him out of

doors,

To wander here and there, like a bad ghost, Because a silly wench refused him—fudge !

Stephen. Most probably. I quite agree with you. Where do you stop ?

Waggoner. A't the first inn we come to ;

You'll see it from the bottom of the hill.

There is a better at the farther end,

But then the stabling is not near so good.

Stephen. I must push on. Four legs can never go Down hill so fast as two. Good morning, friend.

Waggoner. Good morning, sir.

Stephen (aside\'7d. I take the other inn.

SCENE XV.— The Nurse's room. JULIAN and LILIA standing near the window.

Julian. But do you really love me, Lilia ?

Lilia. Why do you make me say it so often,

Julian ?

You make me say I love you, oftener far Than you say you love me.

Julian. Because mine seems

So much a love of mere necessity. I can refrain from loving you no more Than keep from waking when the sun shines full Upon my face.

Lilia. And yet I love to say

How, how I love you, Julian !

[Leans her head on his arm. JULIAN winces a little. She raises her head and looks at him, Did I hurt you?

Would you not have me lean my head on you ? Julian. Come on this side, my love; 'tii a slight hurt Not yet quite healed.

Lilia. Ah, my poor Julian ! how ?

I am so sorry !—Oh ! I do remember! I saw it all quite plain ! It was no dream ! I saw you fighting !—But you did not kill him? Julian (calmly, but drawing himself up\'7d. I

killed him as I would a dog that bit you. Lilia (turning pale, and covering her face unth her hands). Oh, that is dreadful; there is blood on you ! Julian. Shall I go, Lilia ?

So WITHIN AND WITHOUT. PART n.

Lilia. Oh no, no, no, do not. —

I shall be better presently.

Julian. You shrink

As from a murderer.

Lilia. Oh no, I love you —

Will never leave you. Pardon me, my Julian j But blood is very dreadful.

Julian (drawing her close to him\'7d. My sweet

Lilia,

Twas justly shed, for your defence and mine, As it had been a tiger that I killed. He had no right to live. Be at peace, darling; His blood lies not on me, but on himself ; I do not feel its stain upon my conscience.

[A tap at the door.

Enter Nurse.

Nurse. My lord, the steward waits on you,

below. [JULIAN goes.

You have been standing till you're faint, my lady.

Lie down a little. There — I'll fetch you something.

SCENE *XN\.—The Steward's room. JULIAN. The Steward.

Julian. Well, Joseph, that will do. I shall

expect

To hear from you soon after my arrival. Is the boat ready ?

Steward. Yes, my lord j afloat

Where you directed.

Julian, A strange feeling haunts me,

As of some danger near. Unlock it, and cast The chain around the post. Muffle the oars. ft

Steward. I will, directly. [.Goes.

Julian. How shall I manage it ?

I have her father's leave, but have not dared To tell her all; and she must know it first. She fears me half, even now : what will she think VOL. i. o

To see my shaven head'? My heart is free— I know that God absolves mistaken vows. I looked for help in the high search from those Who knew the secret place of the Most High. If I had known, would I have bound myself Brother to men from whose low, marshy minds Never a lark springs to salute the day ? The loftiest of them dreamers ; and the best Content with goodness growing like moss on

stones.

It cannot be God's will I should be such. •But there was more : they "virtually condemned Me in my quest ; would have had me content To kneel with them around a wayside post, Nor heed the pointing finger at its top ? It was the dull abode of foolishness. Not such the house where God would train his

children. My very birth into a world of men

Shows me the school where he would have me

learn;

Shows me the place of penance ; shows the field Where I must fight and die victorious, Or yield and perish. True, I know not how This will fall out : He must direct my way. But then for her—she cannot see all this ; Words will not make it plain ; and if they would, The time is shorter than the words would need : This overshadowing bodes Hearing ill.— It may be only vapour, of the heat Of too much joy engendered ; sudden fear That the fair gladness is too good to live : The wider prospect from the steep hill's crest, The deeper to the gulf the cliff goes down.— But how will she receive it ? Will she think I have been mocking her? How could I help

it?

Her illness and my danger ! But, indeed,

c 2

So strong was I in truth, I never thought
Her doubts might prove a hindrance in the way.
My love did make her so a part of me,
I never dreamed she might judge otherwise,
Until our talk of yesterday. And now
Her horror at Nembroni's death confirms me :
To wed a monk will seem to her the worst
Of crimes which in a fever one might dream.
I cannot take the truth, and, bodily,
Hold it before her eyes. She is not strong.
She loves me not as I love her. But always
— There's Robert for an instance—I have loved
A life for what it might become, far more
Than for its present: there's a germ in her
Of something noble, much beyond her now :
Chance gleams betray it, though she knows it
not. This evening must decide it, come what will.

SCENE XVII. — The inn; the room which had been JULIAN'S. STEPHEN, Host, and
Hostess. Wine on the table.

Stephen. Here, my good lady, let me fill your
glass; Then pass it to your husband, if you please.
Hostess. I thank you, sir ; I hope it's to your
taste ;
My husband's choice is praised. I cannot say I am a judge myself.
Host. I'm confident
It needs but to be tasted.
Stephen (tasting critically, then nodding]. That
is wine.
I quite congratulate you, my good sir, Upon your exquisite judgment.
Host. Thank you, sir.
Stephen (to the Hostess). And so this man, you say, was here until
The night the count was murdered : did he leave Before or after that ?
Hostess. I cannot tell.
He left before it was discovered though. In the middle of the storm, like one possessed,
He rushed into the street, half tumbling me Headlong down stairs. He never came again. He had
paid his bill that morning, luckily ; So joy go with him ! Well, he was an odd one.
Stephen. What was he like, fair Hostess ?
Hostess. Tall and dark*,
And with a lowering look about his brows. He seldom spoke, but, when he did, was civil.
One queer thing was, he always wore his hat, Indoors as well as out. I dare not say He murdered
Count Nembroni; but it was strange He always sat at that same window there, And looked into
the street. 'Tis not as if There were much traffic in this village now ;
These are changed times ; but I have seen the day—
Stephen. Excuse me; you were saying that the
man Sat at the window—
Hostess. Yes ; even after dark

He would sit on, and never call for lights. The first night, I brought candles, as of course ;
He let me set them on the table, true ; But soon's my back was turned, he put them out.

Stephen. Where is the lady ?

Hostess. That's the strangest thing

Of all the story : she has disappeared, As well as he. There lay the count, stone-dead,
White as my apron. The whole house was empty, Just as I told you.

Stephen. Has no search been made ?

Host. The closest search; a thousand pieces offered

For any information that should lead To the murderer's capture. I believe his brother,
Who is his heir, they say, is still in town, Seeking in vain for some intelligence.

Stephen. 'Tis very odd; the oddest thing I've

heard

For a long time. Send me a pen and ink ; I have to write some letters.

Hostess (rising). Thank you, sir,

For your kind entertainment. You'll find ink And paper on that table near the window.
[Exeunt Host and Hostess.

Stephen. We've found the badger's hole ; well draw him next. He couldn't have gone far
with her and not be seen. My life on it, there are plenty of holes and corners in the old house over
the way. Run off with a wench ! Holy brother Julian! Contemptuous brother Julian ! Stand-by-
thyself brother Julian ! Run away with a wench at last !

Well, there's a downfall ! He'll be for marrying her on the sly, and away;—I know the old
fox;— for her conscience-sake, probably not for his. Well, one comfort is, it's damnation and no
reprieve. The ungrateful, atheistical heretic ! As if the good old mother wasn't indulgent enough
to the foibles of her children ! The worthy lady has winked so hard at her dutiful sons, that she's
nearly blind with winking. There's nothing in a little affair with a girl now and then; but to
marry, and knock one's vows on the head! Therein is displayed a little ancestral fact, as to a
certain respectable progenitor, commonly portrayed as the knight of the cloven foot. Keep back
thy servant, &c. —Purgatory couldn't cleanse that ; and more, 'twill never have the chance.
Heaven be about us from harm! Amen. I'll go find the new count. The Church shall have the
castle and estate ; Revenge, in the person of the new count, the body

of Julian; and Stephen may as well have the thousand pieces as not.

SCENE XVIII.— Night. The Nurse's room. LILIA ; to her JULIAN.

Lilia. How changed he is ! Yet he looks very

noble.

Enter JULIAN.

Julian. My Lilia, will you go to England with me?

Lilia. Julian, my father !

Julian. Not without his leave.

He says, God bless us both.

Lilia. Leave him in prison ?

Jiilian. No, Lilia ; he's at liberty and safe, And far from this ere now.

Lilia. You have done this,

My noble Julian. I will go with you To sunset, if you will. My father gone !

Julian, there's none to love me now but you. You will love me, Julian ?—always ?

Julian. I but fear

That your heart, Lilia, is not big enough To hold the love wherewith my heart would fill it.

Lilia. I know why you think that ; and I
deserve it.

But try me, Julian. I was very silly. I could not help it. I was ill, you know ; Or weak at least. May I ask you, Julian, How your arm is to-day ?

Julian. Almost well, child.

'Twill leave an ugly scar, though, I'm afraid.

Lilia. Never mind that, if it be well again.

Julian. I do not mind it ; but when I remember That I am all yours, then I grudge that scratch Or stain should be upon me—soul, body, yours. And there are more scars on me now than I Should like to make you own, without confession.

Lilia. My poor, poor Julian ! Never think of it ;

[Putting her arms round him.

I will but love you more. I thought you had Already told me suffering enough ; But not the half, it seems, of ypnr adventures. You have been a soldier!

Julian. I have fought, my Lilia.

I have been down amongst the horses' feet; But strange to tell, and harder to believe, Arose all sound, unmarked with bruise, or blood Save what I lif.ed from the gory ground.

[Sighing. My wounds are not of such.

[LiLiA, loosening her arms, and drawing back a little with a kind of shrinking, looks a frightened interrogation.

No. Penance, Lilia ; Such penance as the saints of old inflicted Upon their quivering flesh. Folly, I know ; As a lord would exalt himself, by making

His willing servants into trembling slaves. Yet I have borne it.

Lilia (laying hey hand on his arm\'7d. Ah, alas,
my Julian! You have been guilty.

Julian. Not what men call guilty,

Save it be now ; now you will think I sin. Alas, I have sinned much! but not in this. Lilia, I have been a monk.

Lilia. A monk! \'7bTurning $ale.

I thought— \'7bFaltering.

Julian, — I thought you said . . . did you not
say . . . ? \'7bVerypale, brokenly.

I thought you said . . - \'7bWith an effort.

I was to be your wife !

^Covering her face with her hands, and bursting into tears.

Julian (speaking low and in pain\'7d. And so I did.

Lilia (hopefully and looking w). Then you've
had dispensation? . Julian. God has absolved me, though the
Church will not.

He knows it was in ignorance I did it. Rather would he have men to do his will, Than keep a weight of words upon their souls, Which they laid there, not graven by his finger. The vow was made to him—to him I break it. Lilia (weeping bitterly). I would . . . your words were true . . . but I do know . . . It never can . . . be right to break a vow ; • If so, men might be liars every day; You'd do the same by me, if we were married. Jtdlan (in anguish\'7d. 'Tis ever so. Words are the living things !

There is no spirit—save what's born of words ! Words are the bonds that of two souls make one ! Words the security of heart to heart !

God, make me patient ! God, I pray thee, God !

Lttia (not heeding him). Besides, we dare not;

you would find the dungeon Gave late repentance; I should weep away My life within a convent.

Julian. Come to England,

To England, Lilia.

Lilia. Men would point, and say:

There go the monk and his wife; if they, in truth, Called me not by a harder name than that.

Julian. There are no monks in England.

Lilia. But will that

Make right what's wrong ?

Julian. Did I say so, my Lilia ?

I answered but your last objections thus ; I had a different answer for the first.

Lilia. No, no ; I cannot, cannot, dare not do it.

Julian. Lilia, you will not doubt my love j you cannot.

—I would have told you all before, but thought, Foolishly, you would feel the same as I;— I have lived longer, thought more, seen much more ; I would not hurt your body, less your soul, For all the blessedness your love can give: For love's sake weigh the weight of what I say. Think not that must be right which you have heard From infancy—it may

Enter the Steward in haste, £ale, breathless, and bleeding.

Steward. My lord, there's such an uproar in the

town!

They call you murderer and heretic. The officers of justice, with a monk, And the new Count Nembroni, accompanied By a fierce mob with torches, howling out For justice on you, madly cursing you ! They caught a glimpse of me as I returned, And stones and sticks flew round me like a storm;

But I escaped them, old man as I am, And was in time to bar the castle-gates.— Would heaven we had not cast those mounds, and

shut The river from the moat! [Distant yells andcnts.

Escape, my lord ! Julian (calmly). Will the gates hold them out

awhile, my Joseph? Steward. A little while, my lord ; but those

damned torches !

O for twelve feet of water round the walls ! Julian. Leave us, good Joseph; watch them from a window, And tell us of their progress.

[JOSEPH goes. Sounds approach.

Farewell, Lilia !

[Putting his arm round her. She stands like stone Fear of a coward's name shall not detain me. My presence would but bring down evil on you, VOL. r. H

My heart's beloved ; yes, all the ill you fear, The terrible things that you have imaged out If you fled with me. They will not hurt you, If you be not polluted by my presence.

[Light from without flares on the wall.

They've fired the gate. An outburst of mingled cries. Steward (entering). They've fired the gate, my

lord! Julian. Well, put yourself in safety, my dear

Joseph.

You and old Agata tell all the truth, And they'll forgive you. It will not hurt me ; I shall be safe—you know me—never fear.

Steward. God grant it may be so. Farewell,

dear lord ! [Ingoing.

Julian. But add, it was in vain; for the

signora Would not consent; therefore I fled alone.

[LiLiA stands as before.

Steward. It is too true. Good-bye, good-bye, my master ! [Goes.

Julian. Put your arms round me once, my Lilia. What! not once ? not once at parting ?

\Rushingfeet up the stairs, and along the galleries.

O God ! farewell!

[He clasps her to his heart; leaves her; pushes lack the panel, flings open the door, enters, and closes them behind. LILIA starts suddenly from her fixed bewilderment, and flies after him, but forgets to close the sliding panel. Her voice from the inner room, calling.

Lilia. Julian ! Julian !

[The trampling of feet and clamour of -voices. The door of the room is flung open. Enter the foremost of the mob.

1st. I was sure I saw light here. There it is,

burning still. 2nd. Nobody here ! Praise the devil! he minds

his own. Look under the bed, Gian. yd. Nothing there.

H a

. Another door ! Another door ! He'll soon be in hell if he's there. (A she tries to open the door.) The devil had better leave him, to make up the fire at home he'll be cold by and, by. (Rushes into the inner room.\'7d Folio w me, boys !

[The rest follow.

Voices from within. I have him. I have him. Curse your claws ! Why do you fix on me, you crab ? You won't pick up the fiend-spawn so easily, I can tell you. Bring the light there, will you ? (One runs out for the light.) A trap ! a trap ! and a stair, down in the wall ! the hell-faggot's gone ! After him, after him, like storm-drift !

[Sound of descending footsteps. Others rush in with torches and follow.

SCENE XIX.— The river-side, LILIA seated in the boat; JULIAN handing her the bags.

Julian. There, my love—take care,—'tis heavy. Put them right in the middle of the boat : 'Tis excellent ballast.

A loud shout. He steps in and casts the chain loose, then pushes gently off.

Look how the torches gleam Amongst the trees. Thank God, we have escaped!

He rows swiftly off. The torches come nearer, with cries of search.

(In a low tone.) Slip down, my Lilia; lie at full

length

In the bottom of the boat; your dress is white, And would return the torches' glare. I fear The damp night-air will hurt you, dressed like this. _Pulling off his coat, and wrapping her in it.

Now for a strong pull with my muffled oars!

The water mutters Spanish in its sleep. My beautiful! my bride ! my spirit's wife ! God-given, and God-restored ! my heart exults, Dancing round thee, my beautiful! my soul! Once round the headland, I will set the sail; And the fair wind blows right adown the stream. Dear wind, dear stream, dear stars, dear heart of all, White angel lying in my little boat! Strange that my boyhood's skill with sail and helm, Oft steering safely 'twixt the winding banks, Should make me rich with womanhood and life !

[The boat disappears round the headland, J UUAN singing in his heart,

SONG.

Thou hast been blowing leaves, O wind of strife ! Wan, curled, boat-like leaves, that ran and fled; Unresting yet, though folded up from life ; Sleepless, though cast among the unwaking dead.

Out to the ocean fleet and float;
Blow, blow my little leaf-like boat.
O wind of strife ! to us a wedding wind !
O cover me with kisses of her mouth ;
Blow thou our souls together, heart and mind ;
To narrowing northern lines, blow from the south.
Out to the ocean fleet and float;
Blow, blow my little leaf-like boat
Thou hast been blowing many a drifting thing
From circling cove down to the unsheltered sea ;
Thou blowest to the sea my blue sail's wing,
Us to a new love-lit futurity.
Out to the ocean fleet and float, Blow, blow my little leaf-like boat.
END OF PART II.
WITHIN AND WITHOUT.
PART III.
AND weep not, though the Beautiful decay
Within thy heart, as daily in thine eyes ;
Thy heart must have its autumn, its pale skies,
Leading, mayhap, to winter's dim dismay.
Yet doubt not. Beauty doth not pass away ;
Her form departs not, though her body dies.
Secure beneath the earth the snowdrop lies,
Waiting the spring's young resurrection-day,
Through the kind nurture of the winter cold.
Nor seek thou by vain effort to revive
The summer time, when roses were alive ;
Do thou thy work—be willing to be old :
Thy sorrow is the husk that doth infold
A gorgeous June, for which thou need'st not strive.
PART III.
Time : Five years later.
SCENE I.— Night. London. A large meanly furnished room ; a single candle on the table ; a child asleep in a little crib. JULIAN sits by the table, reading in a low voice out of a book. He looks older, and his hair is lined with grey ; his eyes look clearer.

Julian. What is this ? let me see; 'tis called The Singer:

11 Melchah stood looking on the corpse of his son, and spoke not. At length he broke the

silence and said : ' He hath told his tale to the Immortals.' Abdiel, the friend of him that was dead, asked him what he meant by the words ? The old man, still regarding the dead body, spake as follows :—

" Three years ago, I fell asleep on the summit of the hill Yarib ; and there I dreamed a dream. I thought I lay at

the foot of a cliff, near the top of a great mountain ; for beneath me were the clouds, and above me, the heavens deep and dark. And I heard voices sweet and strong; and I lifted up my eyes, and, lo! over against me, on a rocky slope, some seated, each on his own crag, some reclining between the fragments, I saw a hundred majestic forms, as of men who had striven and conquered. Then I heard one say : ' What wouldst thou sing unto us, young man ? A youthful voice replied, tremblingly : ' A song which I have made for my singing.' 'Come, then, and I will lead thee to the hole in the rock : enter and sing.' From the assembly came forth one whose countenance was calm unto awfulness; but whose eyes looked in love, mingled with doubt, on the face of a youth whom he led by the hand towards the spot where I lay. The features of the youth I could not discern : either it was the indistinctness of a dream, or I was not permitted to behold them. And, lo ! behind me was a great hole in the rock, narrow at the entrance, but deep and wide within; and when I looked into it, I shuddered ; for I thought I saw, far down, the glimmer of a star. The youth entered and vanished. His guide strode back to his seat; and I lay in terror near the mouth of the vast cavern. When I looked up once more, I saw all the men leaning forward, with head aside, as if listening intently to a far-off sound. I likewise listened; but, though much nearer than they, I heard nothing. But I could see their faces change like waters in a windy and half-cloudy day. Sometimes, though I heard nought, it seemed to me as if one sighed and prayed beside me ; and once I heard a clang of music

triumphant in hope; but I looked up, and, lo! it was the listeners who stood on their feet and sang. They ceased, sat down, and listened as before. At last one approached me, and I ventured to question him. 'Sir,' I said, 'wilt thou tell me what it means ?' And he answered me thus : ' The youth desired to sing to the Immortals. It is a law with us that no one shall sing a song who cannot be the hero of his tale—who cannot live the song that he sings; for what right hath he else to devise great things, and to take holy deeds in his mouth? Therefore he enters the cavern where God weaves the garments of souls; and there he lives in the forms of his own tale; for God gives them being that he may be tried. The sighs which thou didst hear were his longings after his own Ideal; and thou didst hear him praying for the Truth he beheld, but could not reach. We sang, because, in his first great battle, he strove well and overcame. We await the next.' A deep sleep seemed to fall upon me: and when I awoke, I saw the Immortals standing with their eyes fixed on the mouth of the cavern. I arose and turned towards it likewise. The youth came forth. His face was worn and pale, as that of the dead man before me; but his eyes were open, and tears trembled within them. Yet not the less was it the same face, the face of my son, I tell thee; and in joy and fear I gazed upon him. With a weary step he approached the Immortals. But he who had led him to the cave hastened to meet him, spread forth his arms and embraced him, and said unto him: ' Thou hast told a noble tale; sing to us now what songs thou wilt.' Therefore said

I, as I gazed on my son: ' He hath told his tale to the Immortals." 1
He puts the look down ; meditates awhile ; then rises and walks up and down the room.
And so five years have poured their 'j^ent
streams,
Flowing from fountains in eternity, Into my soul, which, as an infinite gulf, Hath

swallowed them ; whose living caves they
feed;

And time to spirit grows, transformed and kept. And now the day draws nigh when Christ was born \ The day that showed how like to God himself Man had been made, since God could be revealed By one that was a man with men, and still Was one with God the Father ; that men might By drawing nigh to him draw nigh to God, Who had come near to them in tenderness. O God ! I thank thee for the friendly eye, That oft hath opened on me these five years,

Thank thee for those enlightenings of my spirit, That let me know thy thought was towards me ; Those moments fore-enjoyed from future years, Telling what converse I should hold with God. I thank thee for the sorrow and the care, Through which they gleamed, bright phosphorescent sparks

Crushed from the troubled waters, borne on which Through mist and dark my soul draws nigh to
thee.

Five years ago, I prayed in agony That thou wouldst speak to me. Thou wouldst not then,

With that close speech I craved so hungrily. Thy inmost speech is heart embracing heart; And tbou wert all the time instructing me To know the language of thy inmost speech. I thought thou didst refuse, when every hour Thou spakest every word my heart could hear,

Though oft I did not know it was thy voice. My prayer arose from lonely wastes of soul; As if a world far-off in depths of space, Chaotic, had implored that it might shine Straightway in sunlight as the morning star. My soul must be more pure, ere it could hold With thee communion. 'Tis the pure in heart That shall see God. As if a well that lay Unvisited, till water-weeds had grown Up from its depths, and woven a thick mass Over its surface, could give back the sun ! Or, dug from ancient battle-plain, a shield Could be a mirror to the stars of heaven 1 And though I am not yet come near to Him, I know I am more nigh ; and am content To walk a long and weary road to find My Father's house once more. Well may it be A long and weary— I had wandered far. My God, I thank thee, thou dost care for me.

I am content, rejoicing to go on,
Even when my home seems very far away j
For over grief, and aching emptiness,
And fading hopes, a higher joy arises.
In cloudiest nights, one lonely spot is bright,
High overhead, through folds and folds of space j
It is the earnest-star of all my heavens ;
And tremulous in the deep well of my being
Its image answers, gazing eagerly.

Alas, my Lilia !—But I'll think of Jesus, Not of thee now; him who hath led my soul Thus far upon its journey home to God. By poor attempts to do the things he said, Faith has been boni ; free will become a fact j And love grown strong to enter into his, And know the spirit that inhabits there. One day his truth will spring to life in me, And make me free, as God says "I am free." When I am like him, then my soul will dawn VOL. r. i

WITHIN AND WITHOUT. PART lit

With the full glory of the God revealed— Full as to me, though but one beam from him j The light will shine, for I shall comprehend it: In his light I shall see light. God can speak, Yea, will speak to me then, and I shall hear. Not yet like him, how can I hear his words ?

Stopping by the crib, and betiding over the child.

My darling child! God's little daughter, drest In human clothes, that light may thus be clad In shining, so to reach my human eyes ! Come as a little Christ from heaven to earth, To call me father •, that my heart may know "What, father means, and turn its eyes to God! Sometimes I feel, when thou art clinging to me, How all unfit this heart of mine to have The guardianship of a bright thing like thee, Come to entice, allure me back to God By flitting round me, gleaming of thy home, And radiating of thy purity

Into my stained heart j which unto thee Shall ever show the father, answering The divine childhood dwelling hi thine eyes. O how thou teachest me with thy sweet ways, All ignorant of wherefore thou art come, And what thou art to me, my heavenly ward, Whose eyes have drunk that secret place's light, And pour it forth on me ! God bless his own !

[He resumes his walk, singing in a low voice.

My child woke crying from her sleep :

I bended o'er her bed, And soothed her, till in slumber deep

She from the darkness fled.

And as beside my child I stood,

A still voice said in me— " Even thus thy Father, strong and good,

Is bending over thee."

I 2

SCENE II.— Rooms in Lord Seafarers house. A large company ; dattcers ; gentlemen looking on.

1st Gentleman. Henry, what dark-haired queen

is that ? She moves

As if her body were instinct with thought, Moulded to motion by the music's waves, As floats the swan upon the swelling lake; Or as in dreams one sees an angel move, Sweeping on slow wings through the buoyant air, Then folding them, and turning on his track.

2nd. You seem inspired ; nor can I wonder at

She is a glorious woman; and such eyes ! Think—to be loved by such a woman now !
1st. You have seen her, then, before : what is

her name ?

2nd. I saw her once; but could not learn her name.

SCBNB HI. WITHIH AND WITHOUT.

"7

yd. She is the wife of an Italian count, Who for some cause, political I think, Took refuge in this country. His estates The Church has eaten up, as I have heard : Mephisto says the Church has a good stomach.

2nd. How do they live ?

rd. Poorly, I should suppose ;

For she gives Lady Gertrude music-lessons : That's how they know her.—Ah, you should hear her sing!

2nd. If she sings as she looks, or as she

dances, It were as well for me I did not hear.

rd. If Count Lamballa followed Lady Seaford To heaven, I know who'd follow her on earth.

SCENE III.— Julian's room. JULIAN ; LILY asleep.

Julian. I wish she would come home. When the child wakes,

I cannot bear to see her eyes first rest On me, then wander searching through the room ; And then return and rest. And yet, poor Lilia ! 'Tis nothing strange thou shouldst be glad to go From this dull place, and for a few short hours Have thy lost girlhood given back to thee ; For thou art very young for such hard things As poor men's wives in cities must endure.

I am afraid the thought is not at rest, But rises still, that she is not my wife— Not truly, lawfully. I hoped the child Would kill that fancy ; but I fear instead, She thinks I have begun to think the same— Thinks that it lies a heavy weight of sin Upon my heart. Alas, my Lilia ! When every time I pray, I pray that God Would look and see that thou and I be one !

Lily (starting up in her crib). O, take me ! take me !

SCENE in. WITHIN AND WITHOUT.

Julian \'7bgoing up to her with a smile). What is

the matter with my little child ? Lily. I don't know, father; I was very frightened. Julian. 'Twas nothing but a dream. Look—I

am with you. Lily. I am wake now; I know you're there;

but then

I did not know it. [Smiling.

Julian. Lie down then, darling. Go to sleep

again. Lily (beseechingly). Not yet. I will not go to

sleep again j

It makes me so, so frightened. Take me up, And let me sit upon your knee. Where's mother ? I cannot see her.

Julian. She's not at home, my child ;

But soon she will be back.

Lily. But if she walk

Out in the dark streets—so dark, it will catch her

Julian. She will not walk—but t what would

catch her, sweet ? Lily. I don't know. Tell me a story till she

comes.

Julian (taking her, and sitting with her on his knees by the fire). Come then, my little Lily, I will tell you A story I have read this very night.

[She looks in his face.

There was a man who had a little boy. And when the boy grew big, he went and asked His father to give him a purse of money. His father gave him such a large purse full! And then he went away and left his home. You see he did not love his father much.

Lily. Oh! didn't he?—If he had he wouldn't have gone.

Julian. Away he went, far far away he went. Until he could not even spy the top

Of the great mountain by his father's house. And still he went away, away, as if He tried how far his feet could go away ; Until he came to a city huge and wide, Like London here.

Lily. Perhaps it was London.

Julian. Perhaps it was, my child. And there

he spent

All, all his father's money, buying things That he had always told him were not worth, And not to buy them ; but he would and did.

Lily. How very naughty of him !

Julian. Yes, my child.

And so when he had spent his last few pence, He grew quite hungry. But he had none left

To buy a piece of bread. And bread was scarce , Nobody gave him any. He had been Always so idle, that he could not work. But at last some one sent him to feed swine.

Lily. Swine!

Julian. Yes, swine: 'twas all that he could do ;

And he was glad to eat some of their food.

[She stares at him.

But at the last, hunger and waking love Made him remember his old happy home. "How many servants in my father's house Have plenty, and to spare ! " he said. " I'll go And say, ' I have done very wrong, my father ; I am not worthy to be called your son ; Put me among your servants, father, please.' ; Then he rose up and went; but thought the road So much, much farther to walk back again, When he was tired and hungry. But at last He saw the blue top of the great big hill That stood beside his father's house ; and then He walked much faster. But a great way off, His father saw him coining, lame and weary With his long walk j and very different

From what he had been. All his clothes were

hanging

In tatters, and his toes stuck through his shoes—

She bursts into tears.

Lily (sobbing). Like that poor beggar I saw yesterday ?

Julian. Yes, my dear child.

Lily. And was he dirty too ?

Julian. Yes, very dirty ; he had been so long Among the swine.

Lily. Is it all true though, father ?

Julian. Yes, my darling; all true, and truer far Than you can think.

Lily. What was his father like ?

Jtilian. A tall, grand, stately man.

Lily. Like you, dear father ?

Julian. Like me, only much grander.

Lily. 1 love you

The best though. [Kissing him.

Julian. Well, all dirty as he was,

And thin, and pale, and torn, with staring eyes, His father knew him, the first look, far off, And ran so fast to meet him ! put his arms Around his neck and kissed him.

Lily. Oh, how dear!

I love him too ;—but not so well as you.

[Sound of a carnage drawing uj>.

Julian. There is your mother.

Lily. I am glad, so glad J

Enter LILIA, looking pale.

Lilia. You naughty child, why are you not in

bed? Lily (pouting). I am not naughty. I am afraid

to go,

Because you don't go with me into sleep ; And when I see things, and you are not there, Nor father, I am so frightened, I cry out,

And stretch my hands, and so I come awake. Come with me into sleep, dear mother ; come. Lilia. What a strange child it is! There, (kissing her) go to bed. [Laying- her down. Julian (gazing on the child]. As thou art in thy dreams without thy mother, So are we lost in life without our God.

SCENE IV.— LILIA in bed. The room lighted from a gas-lamp in the street; tJie bright shadow of the window on the wall and ceiling.

Lilia. Oh, it is dreary, dreary ! All the time My thoughts would wander to my dreary home. Through every dance, my soul walked evermore In a most dreary dance through this same room. I saw these walls, this carpet; and I heard, As now, his measured step in the next chamber, Go pacing up and down, and I shut out! He is too good for me, I weak for him.

Yet if he put his arms around me once, And held me fast as then, kissed me as then, My soul, I think, would come again to me, And pass from me in trembling love to him. But he repels me now. He loves me, true, — Because I am his wife : he ought to love me j Me, the cold statue, thus he drapes with duty. Sometimes he waits upon me like a maid, Silent with watchful eyes. Oh ! would to Heaven, He used me like a slave bought in the market! Yes, used me roughly ! So, I were his own ; And words of tenderness would falter in, Relenting from the sternness of command. But I am not enough for him : he needs Some high-entranced maiden, ever pure, And thronged with burning thoughts of God and
him.

So, as he loves me not, his deeds for me Lie on me like a sepulchre of stones.

Italian lovers love not so ; but he

Has German blood in those great veins of his.

He never brings me now a little flower.

He sings low wandering sweet songs to the child j

But never sings to me what the voice-bird

Sings to the silent, sitting on the nest.

I would I were his child, and not his wife !

How I should love him then! Yet I have thoughts

Fit to be women to his mighty men ;

And he would love them, if he saw them once.

Ah ! there they come, the visions of my land ! The long sweep of a bay, white sands, and cliffs Purple above the blue waves at their feet. Down the full river comes a light-blue sail; And down the near hill-side come country girls, Brown, rosy, laden light with glowing fruits ; Down to the sands come ladies, young, and clad For holiday ; in whose hearts wonderment At manhood is the upmost, deepest thought \

And to their side come stately, youthful forms,

Italy's youth, with burning eyes and hearts :-—

Triumphant Love is lord of the bright day.

Yet one heart, under that blue sail, would look

With pity on their poor contentedness ;

For he sits at the helm, I at his feet.

He sung a song, and I replied to him.

His song was of the wind that blew us down

From sheltered hills to the unsheltered sea.

Ah ! little thought my heart that the wide sea,

Where I should cry for comforting in vain,

Was the expanse of his wide awful soul,

To which that wind was helpless drifting me t

I would he were less great, and loved me more-

I sung to him a song, broken with sighs,
For even then I feared the time to come :
" O will thine eyes shine always, love, as now ?
And will thy lips for aye be sweetly curved ? "
Said my song, flowing unrhymed from my heart.
" And will thy forehead, ever, sunlike, bend,
And suck my soul in vapours up to thee ?
Ah love ! I need love, beauty, and sweet odours.
Thou livest on the hoary mountains ; I
In the warm valley, with the lily pale,
Shadowed with mountains and its own great
leaves

Where odours are the sole invisible clouds Making the heart weep for deliciousness. Will thy eternal mountain always bear Bide flowers upspringing at the glacier's foot ? Alas ! I fear the storms, the blinding snow, The vapours which thou gatherest round thy head, Wherewith thou shuttest up thy chamber-door, And goest from me into loneliness." Ah me, my song ! it is a song no more ! He is alone amidst his windy rocks ; I wandering on a low and dreary plain !

She weeps herself asleep. VOL. I. K

SCENE V.— LORD SEAFORD, alternately writing at a table and composing at his pianoforte.

SONG.

Eyes of beauty, eyes of light, Sweetly, softly, sadly bright! Draw not, ever, o'er my eye, Radiant mists of ecstasy.

Be not proud, O glorious orbs! Not your mystery absorbs ; But the starry soul that lies Looking through your night of eyes.

One moment, be less perfect, sweet;
Sin once in something small; One fault to lift me on my feet
From love's too perfect thrall I
For now I have no soul; a sea
Fills up my caverned brain, Heaving in silent waves to thee,
The mistress of that main.
O angel ! take my hand in thine ;
Unfold thy shining silver wings ; Spread them around thy face and mine,
Close curtained in their murmurings.
But I should faint with too much bliss
To be alone in space with thee ; Except, O dread ! one angel-kiss
In sweetest death should set me free..
0 beauteous devil, tempt me, tempt me on, Till thou hast won my soul in sighs;
I'll smile with thee upon thy flaming throne, If thou wilt keep those eyes.
And if the meanings of untold desires Should charm thy pain of one faint sting ;
1 will arise amid the scorching fires, I will arise and sing.
O what is God to me ? He sits apart Amidst the clear stars, passionless and cold.
Divine ! thou art enough to fill my heart; O fold me in thy heaven, sweet love, infold.
With too much life, I fall before thee dead.
With holding thee, my sense consumes in storm. Thou art too keen a flame, too hallowed
For any temple but thy holy form.

WITHIN AND WITHOUT. PART ni.

SCBNB VI. — Julian's room next morning; no fire. JULIAN stands at the window, looking into a Lon* donfog.

Julian. And there are mountains on the earth,

far-off;

Steep precipices laved at morn in wind From the blue glaciers fresh ; and falls that leap, Springing from rock to pool abandonedly ; And all the spirit of the earth breathed out, Bearing the soul, as on an altar-flame, Aloft to God. And there is woman-love— Far off, ah me ! [Sitting down wearily.

the heart of earth's delight Withered from mine ! O for a desert sea, The cold sun flashing on the sailing ice-bergs ! Where I might cry aloud on God, until My soul burst forth upon the wings of pain And fled to him, A numbness as of death

Irfolds me. As in sleep I walk. I live,

But my dull soul can hardly keep awake.

Yet God is here as on the mountain-top,

Or on the desert sea, or lonely isle j

And I should know him here, if Lilia loved me,

As once I thought she did. But can I blame

her?

The change has been too much for her to bear. Can poverty make one of two hearts cold, And warm the other with the love of God ? But then I have been silent, often moody, Drowned in much questioning; and she has

thought

That I was tired of her, while more than all I pondered how to wake her living soul. She cannot think why I should haunt my chamber, Except a goaded conscience were my grief ; Thinks not of aught to gain, but all to shun. Deeming, poor child, that I repent me thus

Of that which makes her mine for evermore, It is no wonder if her love grow less. Then I am older much than she j and this Fever, I think, has made me old indeed Before my fortieth year • although, within, I seem as young as ever to myself.

0 my poor Lilia ! thou art not to blame ; I'll love thee more than ever; I will be

So gentle to thy heart where love lies dead ! For carefully men ope the door, and walk With silent footfall through the room where lies, Exhausted, sleeping, with its travail sore, The body that erewhile hath borne a spirit. Alas, my Lilia ! where is dead Love's child ? I must go forth and do my daily work.

1 thank thee, God, that it is hard sometimes To do my daily labour ; for, of old,

When men were poor, and could not bring thee much,

A turtle-dove was all that thou didst ask; And so in poverty, and with a heart Oppressed with heaviness, I try to do My day's work well to thee,—my offering : That he has taught me, who one day sat weary At Sychar's well. Then home when I return, I come without upbraiding thoughts to thee. Ah! well I see man need not seek for penance— Thou wilt provide the lamb for sacrifice; Thou only wise enough to teach the soul, Measuring out the labour and the grief, Which it must bear for thy sake, not its own. He neither chose his glory, nor devised The burden he should bear ; left all to God ; And of them both God gave to him enough. And see the sun looks faintly through the mist; It cometh as a messenger to me. My soul is heavy, but I will go forth ; My days seem perishing, but God yet lives

And loves. I cannot feel, but will believe.

[He rises and is going. LILIA enters, looking weary.

Look, my dear Lilia, how the sun shines out !

Lilia. Shines out indeed ! Yet 'tis not bad for

England. I would I were in Italy, my own ! [Weeps.

Jitlian. 'Tis the same sun that shines in Italy.

Lilia. But never more will shine upon us

there.

It is too late ; all wishing is in vain ! But would that we had not so ill deserved As to be banished from fair Italy!

Julian. Ah! my dear Lilia, do not, do not

think

That God is angry when we suffer ill. 'Twere terrible indeed, if 'twere in anger.

Lilia. Julian, I cannot feel as you. I wish I felt as you feel.

Julian. God will hear you, child,

If you will speak to him. But I must go. Kiss me, my Lilia.

[She kisses him mechanically. He goes "with a sigh. Lilia. It is plain to see

He tries to love me, but is weary of me. [She -weeps.

Enter LILY.

Lily. Mother, have you been naughty? Mother, dear ! \'7bPulling her hand from her face.

SCENE VII.— Julian's room. Noon. LILIA at work; LILY playing in a closet.

Lily \'7brunning up to her mother). Sing me a little song ; please, mother dear.

[LlLlA, looking off her work, and thinking with fixed eyes for a few moments, sings.

SONG.

Once I was a child,

Oime! Full of frolic wild ;

Oime !

All the stars for glancing, All the earth for dancing ; Oime ! Oime !

When I ran about,

Oime! All the flowers came out,

Oime!

Here and there like stray things, Just to be my playthings.

Oime ! Oime !

Mother's eyes were deep,

Oime! Never needing sleep.

Oime!

Morning—they're above me ! Eventide—they love me!

Oime! Oime !

Father was so tall!

Oime! Stronger he than all!

Oime!

On his arm he bore me, Queen of all before me.

Oime! Oime !

Mother is asleep;

Oime! For her eyes so deep,

Oime!

Grew so tired and aching, They could not keep waking.

Oime! Oime !

Father, though so strong,

Oime! Laid him down along—

Oime!

Ey my mother sleeping ; And they left me weeping,

Oime! Oimfe !

Now nor bird, nor bee.

Oime! Ever sings to me !

Oime!

Since they left me crying, All things have been dying.

Oime! Oime!

[LiLY looks long in her mother's face, as if wondering what the song could be about; then turns away to the closet. After a little she comes running with a box in her hand.

Lily. O mother, mother ! there's the old box

I had

So long ago, and all my cups and saucers, And the farm-house and cows.—Oh ! some are broken.

Father will mend them for me, I am sure. I'll ask him when he conies to-night— I will : He can do everything, you know, dear mother.

SCENE VIII. — A merchant's counting-house. JULIAN preparing to go home.

Julian. I would not give these days of common

toil,

This murky atmosphere that creeps and sinks Into the very soul, and mars its hue— Not for the evenings when with gliding keel I cut a pale green track across the west— Pale-green, and dashed with snowy white, and spotted

With sunset crimson ; when the wind breathed

low,

So low it hardly swelled my xebec's sails, That pointed to the south, and wavered not, Erect upon the waters. — Jesus said His followers should have a hundred fold Of earth's most precious things, with suffering. — In all the labourings of a weary spirit, I have been bless'd with gleams of glorious things. The sights and sounds of nature touch my soul, No more look in from far.—I never see Such radiant, filmy clouds, gathered about A gently opening eye into the blue, But swells my heart, and bends my sinking knee, Bowing in prayer. The setting sun, before, Signed only that the hour for prayer was come, Where now it moves my inmost soul to pray. On this same earth He walked ; even thus he

looked

Upon its thousand glories ; read them all; In splendour let them pass on through his soul, And triumph in their new beatitude, Finding a heaven of truth to take them in ; But walked on steadily through pain to death.

Better to have the poet's heart than brain, Feeling than song ; but better far than both, To be a song, a music of God's making ; Or but a table, on which God's finger of flame, In words harmonious, of triumphant verse, That mingles joy and sorrow, sets down clear, That out of darkness he hath called the light. It may be voice to such is after given, To tell the mighty tale to other worlds.

Oh ! I am blest in sorrows with a hope That steeps them all in glory ; as gray clouds Are bathed in light of roses ; yea, I were Most blest of men, if I were now returning To Lilia's heart as presence. O my God,

I can but look to thee. And then the child !— Why should my love to her break out in tears ? Why should she be only a consolation, And not an added joy, to fill my soul With gladness overflowing in many voices Of song, and prayer—and weeping only when Words fainted 'neath the weight of utterance ?

SCENE IX.— . preparing to go out. LILY.

Lily. Don't go to-night again.

Lilia. Why, child, your father

Will soon be home j and then you will not miss me.

Lily. Oh, but I shall though; and he looks so

sad When you're not here.

Lilia (aside). He cannot look much sadder

Than when I am. I am sure 'tis a relief To find his child alone when he returns,

Lily. Will you go, mother ? Then I'll go and

cry

Till father comes. He'll take me on his knee, And tell such lovely tales : you never do — Nor sing me songs made all for my own self. He does not kiss me half so many times As you do, mother j but he loves me more. Do you love father, too ? I love him so ! Lilia (ready). There's such a pretty book ! Sit

on the stool, And look at the pictures till your father comes.

[Goes.

Lily (putting the book down, and going to the window). I wish he would come home. I wish he would.

Enter JULIAN.

Oh, there he is ! [Running up to him.

Oh, now I am so happy ! \'7bLaughing. I had not time to watch before you came.

SCHNE ix. WITHIN AND WITHOUT.

145

Julian (taking her in his arms). I am very glad

to have my little girl ; I walked quite fast to come to her again.

Lily. I do, do love you. Shall I tell you something ?

Think I should like to tell you. 'Tis a dream That I went into, somewhere in last night. I was alone—quite ;—you were not with me, So I must tell you. 'Twas a garden, like That one you took me to, long, long ago, When the sun was so hot. It was not winter, But some of the poor leaves were growing tired With hanging there so long. And some of

them

Gave it up quite, and so dropped down and lay Quiet on the ground. And I was watching them. I saw one falling—down, down—tumbling down — Just at the earth—when suddenly it spread Great wings and flew.—It was a butterfly,

So beautiful with wings, black, red, and white —

\'7bLaughing heartily.

I thought it was a crackly, withered leaf. Away it flew ! I don't know where it went. And so I thought, I have a story now To tell dear father when he comes to Lily.

Julian. Thank you, my child; a very pretty

dream.

But I am tired—will you go find another— Another dream somewhere in sleep for me ? Lily, O yes, I will.—Perhaps I cannot find one.

[He lays her down to sleep ; then sits musing.

Julian. What shall I do to give it life again ? To make it spread its wings before it fall, And lie among the dead things of the earth ?

Lily. I cannot go to sleep. Please, father, sing The song about the little thirsty lily.

[JULIAN smgs e

SCENE ix. WITHIN AND WITHOUT.

SONG.

Little white Lily Sat by a stone, Drooping and waiting Till the sun shone. Little white Lily Sunshine has fed; Little white Lily Is lifting her head.

Little white Lily Said, " It is good : Little white Lily's Clothing and food! Little white Lily Drest like a bride ! Shining with whiteness And crowned beside!"

Little white Lily Droopeth in pain, Waiting and waiting For the wet rain. Little white Lily Holdeth her cup; Rain is fast falling, And filling it up.

Little white Lily Said, " Good again, When I am thirsty To have nice rain ! Now I am stronger, Now I am cool; Heat cannot burn me, My veins are so full !*'

Little white Lily Smells very sweet: On her head sunshine, Rain at her feet 1 ' Thanks to the sunshine! Thanks to the rain ! Little white Lily Is happy again !"

[He fs silent for a moment; then goes and looks at Jier.

Julian. She is asleep, the darling ! Easily Is Sleep enticed to brood on childhood's heart. Gone home unto thy Father for the night!

He returns to his seat.

I have grown common to her. It is strange — This commonness—that, as a blight, eats itp
All the heart's springing corn and promised fruit.

[Looking round.

This room is very common : everything
Has such a well-known look of nothing in it ;
And yet when first I called it hers and mine,
There was a mystery inexhaustible
About each trifle on the chimney-shelf.
But now the gilt is nearly all worn off.
Even she, the goddess of the wonder-world,
Seems less mysterious and worshipful :
No wonder I am common in her eyes.
Alas ! what must I think ? Is this the true ?
Was that the false that was so beautiful ?
Was it a rosy mist that wrapped it round ?
Or was love to the eyes as opium,
Making all things more beauteous than they were?
And can that opium do more than God
To waken beauty in a human brain ?
Is this the real, the cold, undraperied truth;
A skeleton admitted as a guest
At life's loud feast, wearing a life-like mask ?
No, no ; my heart would die if I believed it.

A blighting fog uprises with the days,
False, cold, dull, leaden, gray. It clings about
The present, far dragging like a robe ; but ever
Forsakes the past, and lets its hues shine out:
On past and future pours the light of heaven.
The Commonplace is of the present mind.
The Lovely is the True. The Beautiful
Is what God made. Men from whose narrow
bosoms

The great child-heart has withered, backward look To their first-love, and laugh, and call it folly, A mere delusion to which youth is subject, As childhood to diseases. They know better ; And proud of their denying, tell the youth, On whom the wonder of his being shines, That will be over with him by and by ;

" I was so when a boy—look at me now ! " Youth, be not one of them, but love thy love. So with all worship of the high and good, And pure and beautiful. These men are wiser! Their god, Experience, but their own decay; Their wisdom but the grey hairs gathered on them. Yea, some will mourn and sing about their loss, And for the sake of sweet sounds cherish it, Nor yet believe that it was more than seeming. But he in whom the child's heart hath not died, Hath grown a man's heart, loveth yet the Past; Believes in all its beauty ; knows the hours Will melt the mist; and though this very day Casts but a dull stone on Time's heaped-up cairn, A morning light will break one morn and draw The hidden glories of a thousand hues Out from its crystal-depths and ruby-spots And sapphire-veins, unseen, unknown, before. Far in the future lies his refuge. Time

Is God's, and all its miracles are his ; And in the Future he overtakes the Past, Which was a prophecy of times to come : Tliere lie great flashing stars, the same that shone In childhood's laughing heaven; there lies the
wonder

In which the sun went down and moon arose ; The joy with which the meadows opened out Their daisies to the warming sun of spring; Yea, all the inward glory, ere cold fear Froze, or doubt shook the mirror of his soul. To reach it, he must climb the present slope Of this day's duty—here he would not rest. But all the time the glory is at hand, Urging and guiding—only o'er its face Hangs ever, pledge and screen, the bridal veil: He knows the beauty radiant underneath ; He knows that God who is the living God, The God of living things, not of the dying,

Would never give his child, for God-born love, A cloud-made phantom, fading in the sun. Faith vanishes in sight; the cloudy veil Will melt away, destroyed of inward light.

If thy young heart yet lived, my Lilia, thou And I might, as two children, hand in hand, Go home unto our Father.—I believe It only sleeps, and may be wakened yet.

SCENE X.— Juliarfs room. Christmas Day; early morn. JULIAN.

Julian. The light comes feebly, slowly, to the
world

On this one day that blesses all the year, Just as it comes on any other day : A feeble child he came, yet not the less Brought godlike childhood to the aged earth, Where nothing now is common any more. All things had hitherto proclaimed God :

The wide spread air ; the luminous mist that hid
The far horizon of the fading sea;

The low persistent music evermore
Flung down upon the sands, and at the base
Of the great rocks that hold it as a cup ;
All things most common ; the furze, now golden,
now
Opening dark pods in music to the heat Of the high summer-sun at afternoon ; The lone black tarn upon the round hill-top, O'er which the gray clouds brood like rising
smoke,
Sending its many rills, o'erarched and hid, Singing like children down the rocky sides ;— Where shall I find the most unnoticed thing, For that sung God with all its voice of song ? But men heard not, they knew not God in these ; To their strange speech unlistening ears were
strange;

SCENE x. WITHIN AND WITHOUT.

For with a stammering tongue and broken words,
With mingled falsehoods and denials loud,
Man witnessed God unto his fellow man :
How then himself the voice of Nature hear ?
Or how himself be heeded, when, the leader,
He in the chorus sang in discord vile ?
When prophet lies, how shall the people preach ?
But when He came in poverty, and low,
A real man to half-unreal men,
A man whose human thoughts were all divine,
The head and uptumed face of human kind
Then God shone forth from all the' lowly earth.
And men began to read their maker there.
Now the Divine descends, pervading all.
Earth is no more a banishment from heaven ;
But a lone held among the distant hills,
Well ploughed and sown, whence corn is gathered
home. Now, now we feel the holy mystery
That permeates all being : all is God's ;
And my poor life is terribly sublime.
Where'er I look, I am alone in God,
As this round world is wrapt in folding space ;
Behind, before, begin and end in him :
So all beginnings and all ends are hid ;
And he is hid in me, and I in him.
Oh, what a unity, to mean them all! — The peach-dyed morn ; cold stars in colder blue Gazing across upon the sun-dyed west; While the cold wind is running o'er the graves. Green buds, red flowers, brown leaves, and ghostly
snow;
The grassy hills, breeze-haunted on the brow ; And sandy deserts hung with stinging stars. Half-vanished hangs the moon, with daylight sick, Wan-faced and lost and lonely : daylight fades — Blooms out the pale eternal flower of space, The opal night, whose odours are gray dreams —

Core of its petal-cup, the radiant moon.
All, all the unnumbered meanings of the earth,
Changing with every cloud that passes o'er ;
All, all, from rocks slow-crumbling in the frost
Of Alpine deserts, isled in stormy air,
To where the pool in warm brown shadow sleeps,
The stream, sun-ransomed, dances in the sun ;
All, all, from polar seas of jewelled ice,
To where she dreams out gorgeous flowers — all, all
The unlike children of her single womb —
Oh, my heart labours with infinitude !
All, all the messages that these have borne
To eyes and ears, and watching, listening souls;
And all the kindling cheeks and swelling hearts,
That since the first-born, young, attempting day,
Have gazed and worshipped ! — What a unity,
To mean each one, yet fuse the each in all !
O centre of all forms ! O concord's home !
O world alive in one condensed world !
0 face of Him, in whose heart lay concealed The fountain-thought of all this kingdom of heaven !
Lord, thou art infinite, and I am thine ! I sought my God ; I pressed importunate;
1 spoke to him, I cried, and in my heart
It seemed he answered me. I said—" Oh ! take
Me nigh to thee, thou mighty life of life!
I faint, I die ; I am a child alone
'Mid the wild storm, the brooding desert-night."
" Go thou, poor child, to him who once, like
thee, Trod the highways and deserts of the world."
"Thou sendest me then, wretched, from thy
sight! Thou wilt not have me—I am not worth thy
car,
" I send thee not away ; child, think not so ; From the cloud resting on the mountain-peak,
I call to guide thee in the path by which Thou mayst come soonest home unto my heart. I, I am leading thee. Think not of Him As he were one and I were one ; in him Thou wilt find me, for he and I are one. Learn thou to worship at his lowly shrine, And see that God dwelleth in lowliness." I came to Him; I gazed upon his face ; And lo ! from out his eyes God looked on me !— Yea, let them laugh ! I will sit at his feet, As a child sits upon the ground, and looks Up in his mother's face. One smile from Him, One look from those sad eyes, is more to me Than to be lord myself of hearts and thoughts. O perfect made through the reacting pain In which thy making force recoiled on thee ! Whom no less glory could make visible Than the utter giving of thyself away, Without a thought of grandeur in the deed,
More than a child embracing from full heart!
Lord of thyself and me through the sore grief,
Which thou didst bear to bring us back to God,
Or rather, bear in being unto us

Thy own pure shining self of love and truth !
When I have learned to think thy radiant thoughts,
To love the truth beyond the power to know it,
To bear my light as thou thy heavy cross,
Nor ever feel a martyr for thy sake,
But an unprofitable servant still,—
My highest sacrifice my simplest duty
Imperative and unavoidable,
Less than which All, were nothingness and waste 5
When I have lost myself in other men,
And found myself in thee — the Father then
Will come with thee, and will abide with me.

SCENE XI. — LILIA teaching LADY GERTRUDE. Enter LORD SEAFORD. LILIA rises. He places her a chair, and seats himself at tJte instrument ; plays a low, half-melancholy, half-defiant prelude, and sings.

SONG.

" Look on the magic mirror ;
A glory thou wilt spy : Be with thine heart a sharer,
But go not thou too nigh ; Else thou wilt rue thine error,
With a tear-filled, sleepless eye."
The youth looked on the mirror,
And he went not too nigh; And yet he rued his error,
With a tear-filled, sleepless eye ; For he could not be a sharer
Of what he there did spy.
He went to the magician,
Upon the morrow morn. " Mighty," was his petition,
" Look not on me in scorn ; But one last gaze elysian,
Lest I should die forlorn !"

vol.. i. M

WITHIN AND WITHOUT. PART HI.

He saw her in her glory,
Floating upon the main. Ah me ! the same sad story !
The darkness and the rain ! If I live till I am hoary,
I shall never laugh again.
She held the youth enchanted, Till his trembling lips were pale,
And his full heart heaved and panted To utter all its tale :
Forward he rushed, undaunted— And the shattered mirror fell.

\ffe rises and leaves the room. LU.IA

END OF PART lit,

WITHIN AND WITHOUT.

PART IV.

AND should the twilight darken into night,
And sorrow grow to anguish, be thou strong ;
Thou art in God, and nothing can go wrong
Which a fresh life-pulse cannot set aright.
That thou dost know the darkness, proves the light.

Weep if thou wilt, but weep not all too long ;
Or weep and work, for work will lead to song.
But search thy heart, if, hid from all thy sight,
There lie no cause for beauty's slow decay ;
If for completeness and diviner youth,
And not for very love, thou seek'st the truth ;
If thou hast learned to give thyself away
For love's own self, not for thyself, I say :
Were God's love less, the world were lost, in sooth.

PART IV.

SCENE I.— Slimmer. Julian's room. JULIAN reading out of a book of poems.

Love me, beloved ; the thick clouds lower; A sleepiness filleth the earth and air ; The rain has been falling for many an hour; A weary look the summer doth wear : Beautiful things that cannot be so ; Loveliness clad in the garments of woe.

Love me, beloved ; I hear the birds; The clouds are lighter ; I see the blue; The wind in the leaves is like gentle words Quietly passing 'twixt me and you ; The evening air will bathe the buds With the soothing coolness of summer floods.

Love me, beloved ; for, many a day, Will the mist of the morning pass away ;

Many a day will the brightness of noon Lead to a night that hath lost her moon ; And in joy or in sadness, in autumn or spring, Thy love to my soul is a needful thing.

Love me, beloved ; for thou mayest lie Dead in my sight, 'neath the same blue sky, Love me, O love me, and let me know The love that within thee moves to and fro; That many a form of thy love may be Gathered around thy memory.

Love me, beloved ; for I may lie Dead in thy sight, 'neath the same blue sky ; The more thou hast loved me, the less thy pain, The stronger thy hope till we meet again ; And forth on the pathway we do not know, With a load of love, my soul would go.

Love me, beloved ; for one must lie Motionless, lifeless, beneath the sky ; The pale stiff lips return no kiss To the lips that never brought love amiss ; And the dark brown earth be heaped above The head that lay on the bosom of love.

Love me, beloved ; for both must lie Under the earth and beneath the sky ; The world be the same when we are gone ; The leaves and the waters all sound on ;

The spring come forth, and the wild flowers live,
Gifts-for the poor man's love to give ;
The sea, the lordly, the gentle sea,
Tell the same tales to others than thee ;
And joys, that flush with an inward morn,
Irradiate hearts that are yet unborn ;
A youthful race call our earth their own,
And gaze on its wonders from thought's high throne,
Embraced by fair Nature, the youth will embrace
The maid beside him, his queen of the race ;
When thou and I shall have passed away
Like the foam-flake thou lookedst on yesterday.
Love me, beloved ; for both must tread
On the threshold of Hades, the house of the dead;
Where now but in thinkings strange we roam,

We shall live and think, and shall be at home ;
The sights and the sounds of the spirit land
No stranger to us than the white sea-sand,
Than the voice of the waves, and the eye of the moon,
Than the crowded street in the sunlit noon.
I pray thee to love me, belov'd of my heart;
If we love not truly, at death we part ;
And how would it be with our souls to find
That love, like a body, was left behind !
Love me, beloved ; Hades and Death Shall vanish away like a frosty breath ;
These hands, that now are at home in thine, Shall clasp thee again, if thou still art mine ;
And thou shall be mine, my spirit's bride, In the ceaseless flow of eternity's tide, If the truest love
that thy heart can know Meet the truest love that from mine can flow. Pray God, beloved, for
thee and me, That our souls may be wedded eternally.

\'7bHe closes the book, and is silent for some moments,

Ah me, O Poet ! did thy love last out The common life together every hour ? The slumber
side by side with wondrousness Each night after a day of fog and rain ? Did thy love glory o'er
the empty purse, And the poor meal sometimes the poet's lot ? Is she dead, Poet ? Is thy love
awake?

Alas ! and is it come to this with me ? I might have written that; where am I now ? Yet let
me think : I love less passionately, But not less truly ; I would die for her— A little thing, but all
a man can no.

O my beloved, where the answering love ? Love me, beloved ; whither art thou gone ?
SCENE II. — LilicCs room. LILIA.
Lilia. He grows more moody still, more self-withdrawn.
Were it not better that I went away, And left him with the child ; for she alone Can bring
the sunshine on his cloudy face ? Aias ! he used to say to me, my child. Some convent would
receive me in my land, Where I might weep unseen, unquestioned ; And pray that God, in whom
he seems to dwell, To take me likewise in, beside him there.

Had I not better make one trial first To win again his love to compass me ? Might I not
kneel, lie down before his feet, And beg and pray for love as for my life ? Clasping his knees,
look up to that stern heaven,
That broods above his eyes, and pray for smiles ?
What if endurance were my only meed ?
He would not turn away, but speak forced words,
Soothing with kindness me who thirst for love,
And giving service where I wanted smiles ;
Till by degrees all had gone back again
To where it was, a slow dull misery.
No. 'Tis the best thing I can do for him—
And that I will do—free him from my sight.
In love I gave myself away to him ;
And now in love I take myself again.
He will not miss me ; I am nothing now.
SCENE III.— Lord Seaford'sgarden. LILIA ; LORD SEAFORD.
Lord S. How the white roses cluster on the

trellis !

They look in the dim light as if they floated Within the fluid dusk that bathes them round.

One could "believe that those far distant sounds Of scarce-heard music, rose with the faint scent, Breathed odorous from the heart of the pale

flowers,

As the low rushing from a river-bed, Or the continuous bubbling of a spring In deep woods, turning over its own joy In its own heart luxuriously, alone. 'Twas on such nights, after such sunny days, The poets of old Greece saw beauteous shapes Sighed forth from out the rooted, earth-fast trees, With likeness undefinable retained In higher human form to their tree-homes, Which fainting let them forth into the air, And lived a life in death till they returned. The large-limbed, sweepy-curved, smooth-rinded

beech

Gave forth the perfect woman to the night; From the pale birch, breeze-bent and waving, stole

The graceful, slight-curved maiden, scarcely

grown.

The hidden well gave forth its hidden charm, The Naiad with the hair that flowed like streams, And arms that gleamed like moonshine on wet

sands.

The broad-browed oak, the stately elm, gave forth Their inner life in shapes of ecstasy. All varied, loveliest forms of womanhood Dawned out in twilight, and athwart the grass Half danced with cool and naked feet, half floated Borne on winds dense enough for them to swim. O what a life they lived ! in poet's brain— Not on this earth, alas !—But you are sad; You do not speak, dear lady.

Pardon me.

If such words make me sad, I am to blame. Lord S, Sad ! True, I spoke of lovely, beauteous things ;

Beauty and sadness always go together.
Nature thought Beauty too rich to go forth
Upon the earth without a meet alloy.
If Beauty had been born the twin of Gladness,
Poets had never needed this dream-life ;
Each blessed man had but to look beside him,
And be more blest. How easily could God
Have made our life one consciousness of joy !
It is denied us. Beauty flung around
Most lavishly, to teach our longing hearts
To worship her; then when the soul is full
Of lovely shapes, and all sweet sounds that
breathe,

And colours that bring tears into the eyes— Steeped until saturated with her essence; And, faint with longing, gasps for some one

thing

More beautiful than all, containing all, Essential Beauty's self, that it may say :
" Thou art my Queen—I dare not think to crown
thee,

For thou art crowned already, every part, With thy perfection; but I kneel to thee, The utterance of the beauty of the earth, As of the trees the Hamadryades; I worship thee, intense of loveliness ! Not sea-born only; sprung from Earth, Air,

Ocean,

Star-Fire ; all elements and forms commingling To give thee birth, to utter each its thought Of beauty held in many forms diverse, In one form, holding all, a living Love, Their far-surpassing child, their chosen queen By virtue of thy dignities combined !"— And when in some great hour of wild surprise, She floats into his sight; and, rapt, entranced, At last he gazes, as I gaze on thee, And, breathless, his full heart stands still for joy,

And his soul thinks not, having lost itself

In her, pervaded with her being; strayed

Out from his eyes, and gathered round her form,

Clothing her with the only beauty yet

That could be added, ownness unto him :

Then falls the sternest No with thunder-tone.

Think, lady,—the poor unresisting soul

Clear-burnished to a crystalline abyss

To hold in central deep the ideal form ;

Led then to Beauty, and one glance allowed

From heart of hungry, vacant, waiting shrine,

To set it on the Pisgah of desire—

Lo, the black storm! the slanting, sweeping rain !

Gray distances of travel to no end !

And the dim rush of countless years behind !

[He sinks at her feet.

Yet for this moment, let me worship thee ! Lilia (agitated). Rise, rise, my Icrd this can* not be indeed.

I pray you, cease ; I will not listen to you. Indeed it must not, cannot, must not be ! \'7bMoving as to go.

Lord S. (rising). Forgive me, madam. Let me

cast myself

On your good thoughts. I had been thinking thus, All the bright morning, as I walked alone ; And when you came, my thoughts flowed forth in

words.

It is a weakness with me from my boyhood, That it I act a part in any play, Or follow, merely intellectually, A passion or a motive—ere I know, My being is absorbed, my brain on fire ; I am possessed with something not my own, And live and move and speak in foreign forms. Pity my weakness, madam ; and forgive My rudeness with your gentleness and truth. That you are beautiful is simple fact;

And when I once began to speak my thoughts, The wheels of speech ran on, till they took fire, And in your face flung foolish sparks and dust. I am ashamed ; and but for dread of shame, I should be kneeling now to beg forgiveness.

Lilia. Think nothing more of it, my lord, I pray. —What is this purple flower with the black spot In its deep heart ? I never saw it before.

SCENE IV. — Julian's room. The dusk of evening. JULIAN standing ivith his arms folded, and his eyes fixed on the floor.

Julian. I see her as I saw her then. She sat On a low chair, the child upon her knees, Not six months old. Radiant with motherhood, Her full face beamed upon the face below, Bent over, as with love to ripen love ; Till its intensity, like summer heat, Gathered a mist across her heaven of eyes,

Which grew until it dropt in large slow tears, Rich human rain on furrows of the heart!

[He walks towards the window, seats himself at a little table, and writes.

THE FATHER'S HYMN FOR THE MOTHER TO SING.

My child is lying on my knees ;

The signs of heaven she reads ; My face is all the heaven she sees,

Is all the heaven she needs.

And she is well, yea, bathed in bliss,

If heaven is in my face— Behind it all is tenderness,

And truthfulness and grace.

I mean her well so earnestly, Unchanged in changing mood;

My life would go without a sigh To bring her something good.

I also am a child, and I

Am ignorant and weak ; I gaze upon the starry sky,

And then I must not speak;

SCENE iv. WITHIN AND WITHOUT.

For all behind the starry sky, Behind the world so broad,

Behind men's hearts and .souls doth lie The Infinite of God.

If true to her, though troubled sore,

I cannot choose but be; Thou, who art peace for evermore,

Art very true to me.

If I am low and sinful, bring More love where need is rife;

Tkou knowest what an awful thing It is to be a life.

Hast thou not wisdom to enwrap My waywardness about,

In doubting safety on the lap Of Love that knows no doubt ?

Lo! Lord, I sit in thy wide space, My child upon my knee ;

She looketh up unto my face, And I look up to thee.

N a

SCENE V.— Lord Seaford's house; Lady Gertrude's room. LADY GERTRUDE lying on a couch; LILIA seated beside her, ivith the girl's hand in both hers.

Lady Gertrude. How kind of you to come! And

you will stay

And be my beautiful nurse till I grow well ? I am better since you came. You look so sweet, It brings all summer back into my heart.

Lilia. I am very glad to come. Indeed, I felt No one could nurse you quite so well as I. Lady Gertrude. How kind of you ! Do call me

sweet names now ;

And put your white cool hands upon my head ; And let me lie and look in your great eyes : 'Twill do me good j your very eyes are healing. Lilia. I must not let you talk too much, dear child.

Lady Gei-trude. Well, as I cannot have my music-lesson,

And must not speak much, will you sing to me ? Sing that strange ballad you sang once before; 'Twill keep me quiet.

Lilia. What was it, child ?

Lady Gertrude. It was

Somethipg about a race—Death and a lady—

Lilia. Oh ! I remember. I would rather sing Some other though.

Lady Gertrude. No, no, I want that one. Its ghost walks up and down inside my head, But won't stand long enough to show itself. You must talk Latin to it—sing it away, Or when I'm ill, 'twill haunt me.

Lilia. Well, I'll sing it.

SONG.

Death and a lady rode in the wind, In a starry midnight pale ; Death on a bony horse behind, With no footfall upon the gale.

The lady sat a wild-eyed steed; Eastward he tore to the morn. But ever the sense of a noiseless speed, And the sound of reaping corn!

All the night through, the headlong race Sped to the morning gray ; The dewdrops lay on her cold white face— From Death or the morning ? say.

Her steed's wide knees began to shake, As he flung the road behind ; The lady sat still, but her heart did quake, And a cold breath came down the wind.

When, lo ! a fleet bay horse beside, With a silver mane and tail; A knight, bareheaded, the horse did ride, With never a coat of mail.

He never lifted his hand to Death, And he never couched a spear ; But the lady felt another breath, And a voice was in her ear.

He looked her weary eyes through and through,

With his eyes so strong in faith :

Her bridle-hand the lady drew,

And she turned and laughed at Death.

And away through the mist of the morning gray, The spectre and horse rode wide ; The dawn came up the old bright way, And the lady never died.

Lord Seaford (who has entered during the song). Delightful! Why, my little pining Gertrude,

With such charm-music you will soon be well. Madam, I know not how to speak the thanks I owe you for your kindness to my daughter : She looks as different from yesterday As sunrise from a fog.

Lilia. I am but too happy

To be of use to one I love so much.

SCKNB VI.— A rainy day. LORD SEAFORD walking-up and down his room, murmuring to himself.

Oh, my love is like a wind of death,

That turns me to a slone ! Oh, my love is like a desert breath,

That burns me to the bone !

Oh, my love is a flower with a purple glow,

And a purple scent all day ! But a black spot lies at the heart below,

And smells all night of clay.

Oh, my love is like the poison sweet

That lurks in the hooded cell! One flash in the eyes, one bounding beat,

And then the passing bell !

Oh, my love she's like a white, white rose !

And I am the canker-worm : Never the bud to a blossom blows ;

It falls in the rainy storm.

SCENE VII.— JULIAN reading in his room.

" And yet I am not alone, because the Father is with me."

He closes the book and knects.

SCENE VIII.— Lord Seafords room. LILIA and LORD SEAFORD. Her hand lies in his.

Lilia. It may be true. I am bewildered, though. I know not what to answer. Lord S. Let me answer:—

You would it were so—you would love me then ?

[A sudden crash of music from a brass land in the street, melting away in a low cadence. Lilia (starting up\'7d. Let me go, my lord ! Lord S. (retaining her hand). Why, sweetest! What is this ? Lilia (vehemently, and disengaging her hand).

Let me go ! Oh ! my husband! my pale

child ! [She hurries to the dear, but'falls.

Lord S. (raising her). I thought you trusted me,

yes, loved me, Lilia ! Lilia. Peace ! that name is his ! Speak it again
I rave.

He thought I loved him—and I did—I do. Open the door, my lord !

[He hesitates. She draws herself Tip erect, with flashing eyes.

Once more, my lord—

Open the door, I say.

[He xtill Jiesitates. She walks swiftly to the win* dow, flings it wide, and is throwing herself out.

Lord S. Stop, madam ! I will.

\He opens the door. She leaves tJie window, and •walks slowly out. He Jiears tJte Jiouse-door open and shut, flings himself on the couch, and hides his face.

Enter LADY GERTRUDE.

Lady Gertrude. Dear father, are you ill ? I

knocked three times; You did not speak.

Lord S. I did not hear you, child.

My head aches rather ; else I am quite well.

Lady Gertrude. Where is the countess ?

Lord S. She is gone. She had

An urgent message to go home at once. But, Gertrude, now you seem so well, why not Set out to-morrow ? You can travel now ; And for your sake the sooner that we breathe Italian air the better.

Lady Gertrude. This is sudden ! I scarcely can be ready by to-morrow.

SCENE ix. WITHIN AND WITHOUT. 187

Lord S. It will oblige me, child. Do what you

can.

Just go and order everything you want. I will go with you. Ring the bell, my love ; I have a reason for my haste. We'll have The horses to at once. Come, Gertrude, dear.

SCENE IX.— Evening. Hampstead Heath. LILIA seated.

Lilia. The first pale star of night! the trembling

star!

And all heaven waiting till the sun has drawn His long train after ! then a new creation Will follow their queen-leader from the depths. O leader of new worlds ! O star of love ! Thou hast gone down in me, gone down for ever ; And left my soul in such a starless night, It has not love enough to weep thy loss. O fool ! to know thee once, and, after years, To take a gleaming marsh-light for thy lamp

How could I for one moment hear him speak !

O Julian ! for my last love-gift I thought

To bring that love itself, bound and resigned,

And offering it a sacrifice to thee,

Lead it away into the wilderness;
But one slow spot hath tainted this my lamb ;
Unoffered it must go, footsore and weary
Not flattering itself to die for thee.
And yet, thank God, it was one moment only,
That, lapt in darkness and the loss of thee,
Sun of my soul, and half my senses dead
Through very weariness and lack of love,
My heart throbbed once responsive to a ray
That glimmered through its gloom from other eyes,
And seemed to promise rest and hope again.
My presence shall not grieve thee any more,
My Julian, my husband. I will find
A quiet place where I will seek thy God.
And—in my heart it wakens like a voice

From him—the Saviour—there are other worlds Where all gone wrong in this may be set right; Where I, made pure, may find thee, purer still, And thou wilt love the love that kneels to thee. I'll write and tell him I have gone, and why. But what to say about my late offence, That he may understand just what it was ? For I must tell him, if I write at all. I fear he would discover where I was j Pitiful duty would not let him rest Until he found me ; and I fain would free From all the weight of mine, that heart of his.

[Sound of a coach-Jwrn.
It calls me to rise up and go to him,
Leading me further from him and away.
The earth is round ; God's thoughts return again ;
And I will go in hope. Help me, my God !
SCENE X.— Julian's room. JULIAN redding. A letter is brought in. He reads it, turns deadly pale, and leans his arms and head on the table, almost fainting. This lasts some time; then starting up, he paces through the room, his shoulders slightly shrugged, his arms rigid by his sides, and his hands clenched hard, as if a net of pain were drawn tight around his frame. At length Jie breathes deep, draws himself •up, and walks erect, his chest swelling, but his teeth set.

Julian. Me ! My wife ! Insect, didst thou say
my wife ?
[Hurriedly turning the letter on the table to see the address.
Why, if she love him more than me, why then Let her go with him !—Gone to Italy ! Pursue, says he ? Revenge ? —Let the corpse crush The slimy maggot with its pulpy fingers !— What if I stabbed—
[Taking his dagger, andfeeling its point.
Whom ? Her—what then ?—Or him— What yet ? Would that give back the life to me ?
There is one more—myself! Oh, peace ! to feel The earthworms crawling through my mouldering
brain !—
But to be driven along the windy wastes— To hear the tempests, raving as they turn, Howl Lilia, Lilia —to be tossed about Beneath the stars that range themselves for ever Into the burning letters of her name— 'Twere better creep the earth down here than that ; For pain's excess here sometimes deadens pain.

[*He throws the dagger on thejloor.*

Have I deserved this ? Have I earned it ? I ? A pride of innocence darts through my veins. I stand erect. Shame cannot touch me. Ha ! I laugh at insult. I? I am myself— Why starest thou at me ? Well, stare thy fill; When devils mock, the angels lend their wings :— But what their wings ? I have nowhere to fly. Lilia ! rny worship of thy purity !

Hast thou forgotten—ah ! thou didst not know How, watching by thee in thy fever-pain, When thy white neck and bosom were laid bare, I turned my eyes away, and turning drew With trembling hand white darkness over thee, Because I knew not thou didst love me then. Love me ! O God in heaven ! Is love a thing That can die thus? Love me! Would, for thy

penance, Thou saw'st but once the heart which thou hast

torn—

Shaped all about thy image set within ! But that were fearful! What rage would not, love Must then do for thee—in mercy I would kill thee, To save thee from the hell-fire of remorse. If blood would make thee clean, then blood should

flow;

Eager, unwilling, this hand should make thee bleed, Till, drop by drop, the taint should drop away.

Clean ! said I ? fit to lie by me in sleep, My hand upon thy heart!—not fit to lie, For all thy bleeding, by me in the grave !

His eye falls on tJiat likeness of Jesns said to be copied from an emerald engraved for Tiberius, He gazes, drops on his knees, and covers his

face; remains motionless a long time; then rises very pale, his lips compressed, his eyes filled with tears.

O my poor Lilia ! my bewildered child! How shall I win thee, save thee, make *hee mine ? Where art thou wandering ? What words in thine

ears ?

God, can she never more be clean ? no more, Through all the terrible years? Hast thou no well In all thy heaven, in all thyself, that can Wash her soul clean ? Her body will go down Into the friendly earth—would it were lying There in my arms ; for there thy rains will come, Fresh from the sky, slow sinking through the sod, VOL. i, o

Summer and winter ; and we two should lie Mouldering away together, gently washed Into the heart of earth ; and part would float Forth on the sunny breezes that bear clouds Through the thin air. But her stained soul, my

God ! Canst thou not cleanse it ? Then should we, when

death

Was gone, creep into heaven at last, and sit In some still place together, glory-shadowed. None would ask questions there. And I should be Content to sorrow a little, so I might But see her with the darling on her knees, And know that must be pure that dwelt within The circle of thy glory. Lilia ! Lilia ! I scorn the shame rushing from head to foot; I would endure it endlessly, to save One thought of thine from his polluting touch j Saying ever to myself : this is a part

Of my own Lilia ; and the world to me

Is nothing since I lost the smiles of her :

Somehow, I know not how, she faded from me,

And this is all that's left of her. My wife !

Soul of my soul! my oneness with myself!

Come back to me ; I will be all to thee :

Back to my heart; and we will weep together,
And pray to God together every hour,
That he would show how strong he is to save.
The One that made is able to renew :
I know not how.—I'll hold thy heart to mine,
So close that the defilement needs must go.
My love shall ray thee round, and, strong as fire,
Dart through and through thy soul, till it be
cleansed.—
But if she love him ? Oh my heart—beat! beat! Grow not so sick with misery and life,
For fainting will not save thee.—Oh no ! no 1 She cannot love him as she must love me.
Then if she love him not, oh horrible oh God ! [He stands in a stumor for some minutes.
What devil whispered that vile word, unclean ?
I care not—loving more than that can touch.
Let me be shamed, ay, perish in my shame,
As men call perishing, so she be saved.
Saved ! my beloved ! my Lilia ! alas !
Would she were here, and I would make her weep,
Till her soul wept itself to purity.
Far, far away ! where my love cannot reach. No, no; she is not gone.
[Starting and pacing wildly through the room.
It is a lie—
Deluding blind revenge, not keen-eyed love. I must do something.— [Enter \MX.
Ah! there's the precious thing That shall entice her back.
[Kneeling and clasping the child to his heart.
My little Lily,
1 have lost your mother.
Lily. Oh ! [Beginning to weep,
She was so pretty, Somebody has stolen her.
'Julian. Will you go with me,
And help me look for her ? Lily. O yes, I will.
[Clasping him round the neck.
But my head aches so ! Will you carry me ? Julian. Yes, my own darling. Come, we'll get
your bonnet. Lily. Oh! you've been crying, father. You're
SO white ! [Putting her finger to his cheek.
SCENE XI.— A table in a club-roo»i. Several Gentlemen seated round it. To them enter
another,
1st Gentleman. Why, Bernard, you look heated: what's the matter ?
Bernard. Hot work, as looked at; cool enough,
as done.
2nd G. A good antithesis, as usual, Bernard. 'But a shell too hard for the vulgar teeth Of
our impatient curiosity.
Barnard. Most unexpectedly I found myself Spectator of a scene in a home-drama Worth
all stage-tragedies I ever saw. AIL What was it ? Tell us then. Here, take this seat. He sits at the
talk, and pours out a glass of wine.
Bernard. I went to call on Seaford, and was told He had gone to town. So I, as privileged,

Went to his cabinet to write a note ; Which finished, I came down, and called his valet. Just as I crossed the hall I heard a voice— " The Countess Lamballa—is she here to-day ? " And looking towards the door I caught a glimpse Of a tall figure, gaunt and stooping, drest

In a blue shabby frock down to his knees,
And on his left arm sat a little child.
The porter gave short answer, with the door
For period to the same ; when, like a flash,
It flew wide open, and the serving man
Went reeling, staggering backward to the stairs,
'Gainst which he fell, and, rolling down, lay
stunned.

In walked the visitor; but in the moment Just measured by the closing of the door, Heavens! what a change! He walked erect, as if Heading a column, with an eye and face As if a fountain-shaft of blood had shot Up suddenly within his wasted frame. The child sat on his arm quite still and pale, But with a look of triumph in her eyes. Of me he took no notice; came right on ; Looked in each room that opened from the hall ; In every motion calm as glacier's flow,

Save, now and then, a movement, sudden, quick, Of his right hand across to his left side: 'Twas plain he had been used to carry arms.

yd G. Did no one stop him ?

Bernard. Stop him ? I'd as soon

Have faced a tiger with bare hands. 'Tis easy In passion to meet passion; but it is A daunting thing to look on, when the blood Is going its wonted pace through your own veins. Besides, this man had something in his face, With its live eyes, close lips, nostrils distended, A self-reliance, and a self-command, That would go right up to its goal, in spite Of any no from any man. I would As soon have stopped a cannon-ball as him. Over the porter, lying where he fell, He strode, and up the stairs. I heard him go— I listened as it were a ghost that walked With pallid spectre-child upon its arm—

Along the corridors, from door to door, Opening and shutting. But at last a sting Of sudden fear lest he should find the lady, And mischief follow, shot me up the stairs. I met him half-way down, quiet as at first ; The fire had faded from his eyes ; the child Held in her tiny hand a lady's glove Of delicate primrose. When he reached the ha?!, He turned him to the porter, who had scarce Lifted him from the floor, and saying thus : "The Count Lamballa waited on Lord Seaford,' Turned him again, and strode into the street. 1st G. Have you got hold of any clue ? Bernard. Not any.

Of course he had suspicions of his wife : For all the gifts a woman has to give, I would not rouse such blood. And yet to see The gentle faiiy child fall kissing him, And, w»th her little arms grasping his neck,

Peep anxious round into his shaggy face,
As they went down the street!—it almost made
A fool of me.—I'd marry for such a child !

SCENE XII.— A by-street. JULIAN walking home very weary. The child in his arms, her head lying on his shoulder. An Organ-boy with a monkey, sitting on a door-stefi. He sings in a low -voice.

Julian. Look at the monkey, Lily. Lily. No, dear father ;
I do not like monkeys.
Julian. Hear the poor boy sing.

Tfiey listen. He sings.

SONG.

Wenn ich liore dich mir nah', Stimmen in den Blattern da ; Wenn ich fuhl' dich weit und breit, Vater, das ist Seligkeit.

Nun die Sonne liebend scheint, Mich mit dir und All vereint; Biene zu den Blumen fliegt, Seel' an Lieb' sich liebend schmiegt.

SCUNE xn. WITHIN AND WITHOUT.

So mich vollig lieb du hasl, Daseyn ist nicht eine Last; Wenn ich seh' und hore dich, Das genugt mir inniglich.

Lily. It sounds so curious. What is lie saying,

father ?

Julian. My boy, you are not German ? Boy. No ; my mother

Came from those parts. She used to sing the

song. I hardly understand it all myself,

For I was born in Genoa.—Ah! my mother!

[Weeps.

Julian. My mother was a German, my poor boy; My father was Italian : I am like you.
Giving him money.

You sing of leaves and sunshine, flowers and bees, Poor child, upon a stone in the dark street ?

Boy. My mother sings it in her grave; and I Will sing it everywhere, until I die.

SCENE XIII.— LILIA'S room. JULIAN enters with the child; -undresses her, and puts her to bed.

Lily. Father does all things for his little Lily. Julian. Dear, dear Lily ! Go to sleep, my pet. [Sitting' by her.

" Wenn ich seh' und h5re dich, Das genligt mir inniglich."_ Falling on his knees,

I come to thee, and, lying on thy breast, Father of me, I tell thee in thine ear, Half-shrinking from the sound, yet speaking free, That thou art not enough for me, my God. Oh, dearly do I love thee ! Look : no fear Lest thou shouldst be offended, touches me. Herein I know thy love : mine casts out fear. O give me back my wife ; thou without her Canst never make me blessed to the full. \Silence*

O yes; thou art enough for me, my God; Part of thyself she is, else never mine.

My need of her is but thy thought of me; She is the offspring of thy beauty, God j Yea of the womanhood that dwells in thee : Thou wilt restore her to my very soul. [Rising.

It may be all a lie. Some needful cause Keeps her away. Wretch that I am, to think One moment that my wife could sin against me ! She will come back to-night. I know she will. How shall I answer for such jealousy ! For that fool-visit to Lord Seaford's house !

[His eyes fall on tJie glove "which the child still Jwlds in her sleeping hand. He takes it gently away, and hides it in his bosom.

It will be all explained. To think I should, Without one word from her, condemn her so ! What can I say to her when she returns ? I shall be utterly ashamed before her. She will come back to-night. I know she will.

[He throws himself wearily on the bed.

SCENE XIV.— Crowd about the Italian OJ>era-Hoitst. JULIAN. LILY in his arms.
Three Students.

st StTidettt. Edward, you see that long, lank,

threadbare man ?

There is a character for that same novel You talk of thunder-striking London with, One of these days.

2nd Sf. I scarcely noticed him;

I was so taken with the lovely child. She is angelic.

St. You see angels always,

Where others, more dim-sighted, see but mortals. She is a pretty child. Her eyes are splendid. I wonder what the old fellow is about. Some crazed enthusiast, music-distract, That lingers at the door he cannot enter! Give him an obol, Frank, to pay old Charon,

And cross to the Elysium of sweet sounds. Here's mine.

1st St. And mine.

2nd St. And mine.

[yd Student offers the money to JULIAN.

Julian (very quietly\'7d. No, thank you, Sir.

Lily, Oh ! there is mother !

[Stretching her hands towards a lady stepping out of a carriage.

Julian. No, no ; hush, my child !

TJie lady looks round, and LILY clings to her father. Women talking.

1st W. I'm sure he's stolen the child. She can't

be his.

2nd W. There's a suspicious look about him. $d W. True;

But the child clings to him as if she loved him.

[JULIAN moves on slo^vly.

SCENE XV.— JULIAN seated in his room, his eyes fixed on the floor. LILY play ing in a corner*

Julian. Though I am lonely, yet this little

child-She understands me better than the Twelve Knew the great heart of him they called their Lord.

Ten times last night I woke in agony, I knew not why. There was no comforter. I stretched my arm to find her, and her place Was empty as my heart. Though wide awake, Sometimes my pain, benumbed by its own being, Forgets its cause, and I would lay my head Upon her breast—that promises relief : I lift my eyes, and lo, the vacant world !

He looks up and sees the child playing ivith his dagger.

You'll hurt yourself, my child ; it is too sharp. Give it to me, my darling. Thank you, clear.

[? brealiS the hilt from the blade and gives it her.

Here, take the pretty part. It's not so pretty

As it was once— [Thinking aloud.

I picked the jewels out

To buy your mother the last dress I gave her. There's just one left, I see, for you, my Lily. Why did I kill Nembroni ? Poor saviour I, Leading thee only to a greater ill!

If thou wert dead, the child would comfort

me;—

Is she not part of thee, and all my own ? But now

Lily (throwing down the dagger-hilt, and running up to hijii). Father, what is a poetry ?

Julian. A beautiful thing,—of the most beautiful That God has made.

Lily. As beautiful as mother ?

Julian. No, my dear child ; but very beautiful.

Lily. Do let me see a poetry.

Julian (opening a book\'7d. There, love.

VOL. I. p

210 -

Lily (disappointedty>). I don't think that's so

very pretty, father. One side is very well—smooth ; but the other

[Rulling her finger nj> and down the ends of the lines.

Is rough, rough; just like my hair in the morning, [Smoothing her hair down with both hands.

Before it's brushed. I don't care much about it. 'Julian (putting the book down, and taking her on his knee). You do not understand it yet, my child.

You cannot know where it is beautiful. But though you do not see it very pretty, Perhaps your little ears could hear it pretty.

[He reads. Lily (looking pleased]. Oh ! that's much prettier,

father. Very pretty.

It sounds so nice !—not half so pretty as mother. Julian. There's something in it very beautiful, If I could let you see it. When you're older

You'll find it for yourself, and love it well. Do you believe me, Lily ? Lily. Yes, dear father.

ten looking at the look, I wonder where its prettiness is, though; I cannot see it anywhere at all.

He sets her down. She goes to Jier corner.

Julian (musing). True, there's not much in me

to love, and yet

I feel worth loving. I am very poor, But that I could not help; and I grow old, But there are saints in heaven older than I. I have a world within me ; there I thought I had a wealth of lovely, precious things, — Laid up for thinking; shady woods, and grass ; Clear streams rejoicing down their sloping

channels;

And glimmering daylight in the cloven east; There morning sunbeams stand, a vapoury column,

P 2

'Twixt the dark boles of solemn forest trees ; There, spokes of the sun-wheel, that cross their

bridge, Break through the arch of the clouds, fall on the

earth,

And travel round, as the wind blows the clouds : The distant meadows and the gloomy river Shine out as over them the ray-pencil sweeps.— Alas ! where am I ? Beauty now is torture : Of this fair world I would have made her queen ;— Then led her through the shadowy gates beyond Into that farther world of things unspoken, Of which these glories are the outer stars. The clouds that float within its atmosphere. Under the holy might of teaching love, I thought her eyes would open —see how, far And near, Truth spreads her empire, widening out, And brooding, a still spirit, everywhere; Thought she would turn into her spirit's chamber,

      Open the little window, and look forth

      On the wide silent ocean, silent winds,

      And see what she must see, I could not tell.

      By sounding mighty chords I strove to wake

      The sleeping music of her poet-soul:

      We read together many magic words j

      Gazed on the forms and hues of ancient art;

      Sent forth our souls on the same tide of sound ;

      Worshipped beneath the same high temple-roofs ;

      And evermore I talked. I was too proud,

      Too confident of power to waken life,

      Believing in my might upon her heart,

      Not trusting in the strength of living truth.

      Unhappy saviour, who by force of self

      Would save from selfishness and narrow needs

      I have not been a saviour. She grew weary.

      J began wrong. The infinitely High,

      Made manifest in lowliness, had been

      The first, one lesson. Had I brought her there,

      And sei her down by humble Mary's side, He would have taught her all I could not teach.

Yet, O my God ! why hast thou made me thus Terribly wretched, and beyond relief?

      He looks up and sees that tJte child has taken the book to her corner. She peefs into it;

then holds it to her ear', then rubs her hand over it; then puts her tongue on it.

      Julian (bursting into tears\'7d. Father, I am thy

      child. Forgive me this : Thy poetry is very hard to read.

      SCENE XVI.— JULIAN walking with LILY through one of the squares.

      Lily. Wish we could find her somewhere. 'Tis

      so sad

      Not to have any mother ! Shall I ask This gentleman if he knows where she is ?

      Julian. No, no, my love; we'll find her by and by.

      BERNARD and another Gentleman talking togetfar.

      Bernard. Have you seen Seaford lately ?

      Gentleman. No. In fact,

      He vanished somewhat oddly, days ago. Sam saw him with a lady in his cab ; And if I

hear aright, one more is missing— Just the companion for his lordship's taste. You've not forgot

that fine Italian woman You met there once, some months ago ?

      Bern, Forgot her !

      I have to try though, sometimes—hard enough.

      Lily. Mother was Italy, father—was she not ?

      Julian. Hush, hush, my child ! you must not say a word.

      Bern. Her husband is alive.

      Gentleman. Oh, yes ! he is ;

      But what of that—a poor half-crazy creature !

      Bern. Something quite different, I assure you, Harry,

      Last week I saw him—never to forget him— Ranging through Seaford's house, like the questing beast. Gentleman. Better please two than one, they

thought, no doubt.

I am not the one to blame him ; she is a prize Worth sinning for a little more than little.

Lily whispering). Why don't you ask them

whether it was mother ? I am sure it was. I am quite sure of it. Gentleman. Look what a lovely child ! Bern. Henry ! Good heavens !

It is the Count Lamballa. Come along.

SCENE XVII.— Julian's room. JULIAN. LILY asleep.

Julian. I thank thee. Thou hast comforted

me, thou, To whom I never lift my soul, in hope

To reach thee with my thinking, but the tears

Swell up and fill my eyes from the full heart

That cannot hold the thought of thee, the thought

Of him in whom I live, who lives in me,

And makes me live in him ; by whose one thought,

Alone, unreachable, the making thought,

Infinite and self-bounded, I am here,

A living, thinking will, that cannot know

The power whereby I am—so blest the more

In being thus in thee—Father, thy child.

I cannot, cannot speak the thoughts in me.

My being shares thy glory : lay on me

What thou wouldst have me bear. Do thou

with me

Whate'er thou wilt. Tell me thy will, that I May do it as my best, my highest joy; For thou dost work in me, I dwell in thee.

Wilt thou not save my wife ? I cannot know The power in thee to purify from sin.

But Life can cleanse the life it lived alive. Thou knowest all that lesseneth her fault. She loves me not, I know—ah ! my sick heart!— I will love her the more, to fill the cup ; One bond is snapped, the other shall be doubled ; For if I love her not, how desolate The poor child will be left! he loves her not. I have but one prayer left to pray to thee— Give me my wife again, that I may watch And weep with her, and pray with her, and tell What loving-kindness I have found in thee ; And she will come to thee to make her clean. Her soul must wake as from a dream of bliss, To know a dead one lieth in the house : Let me be near her in that agony, To tend her in the fever of the soul, Bring her cool waters from the wells of hope, Look forth and tell her that the morn is nigh ; And when I cannot comfort, help her weep.

God, I would give her love like thine to me, Because I love her, and her need is great. Lord, I need her far more than thou need'st me, And thou art Love down to the deeps of hell: Help me to love her with a love like thine.

How shall I find her ? It were horrible If the dread hour should come, and I not near. Yet pray I not she should be spared one pang, One writhing of self-loathing and remorse; For she must hate the evil she has done. Only take not away hope utterly. Lily (in her sleep\'7d. Lily means me—don't throw it over the wall.

Julian (going to her). She is so flushed ! I fear

the child is ill.

I have fatigued her too much, wandering restless. To-morrow I will take her to the sea.

[Returning.

If I knew where, I'd write to her, and write So tenderly, she could not choose but come.

I will write now ; I'll tell her that strange dream I dreamed last night: 'twill comfort her as well.

[He sits down and writes.

My heart was crushed that I could hardly
breathe.

I was alone upon a desolate moor ; And the wind blew by fits and died away— I know not if it was the wind or me. How long I wandered there, I cannot tell; But some one came and took me by the hand. I gazed but could not see the form that led me, And went unquestioning, I cared not whither. We came into a street I seemed to know, Came to a house that I had seen before. The shutters were all closed ; the house was dead. The door went open soundless. We went in, And entered yet again an inner room. The darkness was so dense, I shrunk as if From striking on it. The door closed behind.

And then I saw that there was something black, Dark in the blackness of the night, heaved up In the middle of the room. And then I saw That there were shapes of woe all round the room, Like women in long mantles, bent in grief, With long veils hanging low down from their
heads,

All blacker in the darkness. Not a sound Broke the death-stillness. Then the shapeless thing Began to move. Four horrid muffled figures Had lifted, bore it from the room. We followed, The bending woman-shapes, and I. We left The house in long procession. I was walking Alone beside the coffin—such it was— Now in the glimmering light I saw the thing. And now I saw and knew the woman-shapes : Undine clothed in spray, and heaving up White arms of lamentation ; Desdemona In her night-robe, crimson on the left side ;

Thekla in black, with resolute white face ; And Margaret in fetters, gliding slow— That last look, when she shrieked on Henry, frozen Upon her face. And many more I knew— Long-suffering women, true in heart and life ; Women that make man proud for very love Of their humility, and of his pride Ashamed. And in the coffin lay my wife.

On, on, we went. The scene changed. For
the hills

Began to rise from either side the path. At last we came into a narrow glen, From which the mountains rose abrupt to heaven, Shot cones and pinnacles into the skies. Upon the eastern side one mighty summit Shone with its snow faint through the dusky air. Upon its sides the glaciers gave a tint, A dull metallic gleam, to the slow night.

From base to top, on climbing peak and crag,

Ay, on the glaciers' breast, were human shapes, Motionless, waiting ; men that trod the earth Like gods ; or forms ideal that inspired Great men of old—up, even to the apex Of the snow-spear-point. Morning had arisen From Chilian's tomb in Florence, where the chisel Of Michelagnolo laid him reclining, And stood upon the crest.

A cry awoke
Amid the watchers at the lowest base, And swelling rose, and sprang from mouth to
mouth,

Up the vast mountain, to its aerial top ; And "Is God coming? " was the cry ; which died Away in silence ; for no voice said No,

The bearers stood and set the coffin down ; The mourners gathered round it in a group ; Somewhat apart I stood, I know not why

So minutes passed. Again that cry awoke,
And clomb the mountain-side, and died away In the thin air, far-lost. No answer came.
How long we waited thus, I cannot tell— How oft the cry arose and died again.

At last, from far, faint summit to the base, Filling the mountain with a throng of echoes, A mighty voice descended : " God is coming I " Oh ! what a music clothed the mountain-side, From all that multitude's melodious throats, Of joy and lamentation and strong prayer ! It ceased, for hope was too intense for song. A pause.—The figure on the crest flashed out, Bordered with light. The sun was rising—rose Higher and higher still. One ray fell keen Upon the coffin 'mid the circling group.

What God did for the rest, I know not; it Was easy to help them.—I saw them not.— I saw thee at my feet, my wife, my own ! Thy lovely face angelic now with grief;

But that I saw not first: thy head was bent, Thou on thy knees, thy dear hands clasped between. I sought to raise thee, but thou wouldst not rise, Once only lifting that sweet face to mine, Then turning it to earth. Would God the dream Had lasted ever !—No ; 'twas but a dream ; Thou art not rescued yet.

Earth's morning came, And my soul's morning died in tearful gray. The last I saw was thy white shroud yet steeped In that sun-glory, all-transfiguring. And as a slow chant blossomed suddenly Into an anthem, silence took me like sound : I had not listened in the excess of joy.

SCENE XVIII.— Portsmouth. A bedroom. LORD SEA-FORD. LADY GERTRUDE.

Lord S. 'Tis for your sake, my Gertrude, I am sorry.

VOL. I. Q

If you could go alone, I'd have you go.

Lady Gertrude. And leave you ill ? No, you
are not so cruel.

Believe me, father, I am happier In your sick room, than on a glowing island In the blue Bay of Naples.

Lord S. It was so sudden !

I fear it will not go again as quickly. But have your walk before the sun be hot. Put the ice near me, child. There, that will do.

Lady Gertrude. Good-bye then, father, for a little while. [Goes.

Lord S. I never knew what illness was before. O life ! to think a man should stand so little On his own will and choice, as to be thus Cast from his high throne suddenly, and sent To grovel beast-like. All the glow is gone From the rich world ! No sense is left me more To touch with beauty. Even she has faded

Into the far horizon, a spent dream Of love and loss and passionate despair Is there no beauty ? Is it all a show Flung outward from the healthy blood and nerves, A reflex of well-ordered organism ? Is earth a desert ? Is a woman's heart No more mysterious, no more beautiful, Than I am to myself this ghastly moment ? It must be so—it must, except God is, And means the meaning that we think we see, . Sends forth the beauty we are taking in. O Soul of nature, if thou art not, if There dwelt not in thy thought the primrose-flower

Before it blew on any bank of spring, Then all is untruth, unreality, And we are wretched things ; our highest needs Are less than we, the offspring of ourselves ; And when we are sick, they are not; and our hearts

Q a

Die with the voidness of the universe. But if thou art, O God, then all is true ; Nor are thy thoughts less radiant that our eyes Are filmy, and the weary, troubled brain Throbs in an endless round of its own dreams. And she is beautiful and I have lost her!

O God ! thou art, thou art; and I have sinned Against thy beauty and thy graciousness ! That woman-splendour was not mine, but thine. Thy thought passed into form, that glory passed Before my eyes, a bright particular star : Like foolish child, I reached out for the star, Nor kneeled, nor worshipped. I will be content That she, the Beautiful, dwells on in thee, Mine to revere, though not to call my own. Forgive me, God ! Forgive me, Lilia !

My love has taken vengeance on my love. I writhe and moan. Yet I will be content. Yea gladly will I yield thee, so to find

That thou art not a phantom, but God's child ;

That Beauty is, though it is not for me.

When I would hold it, then I disbelieved :

That I may yet believe, I will not touch it.

I have sinned against the Soul of love and beauty,

Denying him in grasping at his work.

SCENE XIX.— A country church-yard. JULIAN seated on a tombstone. LILY gatJiering flowers and grass among- tJic graves.

Julian. O soft place of the earth ! down-pillowed

couch,

Made ready for the weary ! Everywhere, O Earth, thou hast one gift for thy poor children— Room to lie down, leave to cease standing up Leave to return to thee, and in thy bosom Lie in the luxury of primeval peace, Fearless of any morn ; as a new babe Lies nestling in his mother's arms in bed :

That home of blessedness is all there is ; He never feels the silent rushing tide, Strong setting for the sea, which bears him on, Unconscious, helpless, to wide consciousness. But thou, thank God, hast this warm bed at last Ready for him when weary : well the green Close-matted coverlid shuts out the dawn. O Lilia, would it were our wedding bed To which I bore thee with a nobler joy ! —Alas ! there's no such rest: I only dream Poor pagan dreams with a tired Christian brain. How couldst thou leave me, my poor child?

my heart

Was all so tender to thee 1 But I fear My face was not. Alas ! I was perplexed With questions to be solved, before my face Could turn to thee in peace : thy part in me Fared ill in troubled workings of the brain. Ah, now I know I did not well for thee

In making thee my wife. I should have gone

Alone into eternity. I was

Too rough for thee, for any tender woman—

Other I had not loved—so full of fancies !

Too given to meditation. A deed of love

Is stronger than a metaphysic truth ;

Smiles better teachers than the mightiest words.

Thou, who wast life, not thought, how couldst

thou help it ?

How love me on, withdrawn from all thy sight— For life must ever need the shows of life ? How fail to love a man so like thyself, Whose manhood sought thy fainting womanhood? I brought thee pine-boughs, rich in hanging

cones,

But never white flowers, rubied at the heart: O God, forgive me ; it is all my fault. Would

I have had dead Love, pain-galvanized, Led fettered after me by gaoler Duty ?

Thou gavest me a woman rich in heart, And I have kept her like a caged sea-mew Starved by a boy, who weeps when it is dead.

0 God, my eyes are opening—fearfully :

1 know it now—'twas pride, yes, very pride That kept me back from speaking all my soul. I was self-haunted, self-possessed—the worst Of all possessions. Wherefore did I never Cast all my being, life and all, on hers,

In burning words of openness and truth ?
Why never fling my doubts, my hopes, my love,
Prone at her feet abandonedly ? Why not
Have been content to minister and wait;
And if she answered not to my desires,
Have smiled and waited patient ? God, they say,
Gives years a hundred to an aloe-flower :
I gave not five years to a woman's soul.
Had I not drunk at last old wine of love?
I flung her love back on her lovely heart ;
I did not shield her in the wintry day ;
And she has withered up and died and gone.
God, let me perish, so thy beautiful
Be brought with gladness and with singing home.
If thou wilt give her back to me, I vow
To be her slave, and serve her with my soul.
I in my hand will take my heart, and burn
Sweet perfumes on it to relieve her pain.
I, I have ruined her—O God, save thou !

\'7bHe bends his head upon his knees. LILY comes running up to him, stumbling over the graves.

Lily. Why do they make so many hillocks,
father ?
The flowers would grow without them. Jtilian. So they would.
Lily. What are they for, then ? Julian (aside). I wish I had not
brought her; She will ask questions. I must tell her all.
(Aloud.) 'Tis where they lay them when the story's
done.
Lily. What! lay the boys and girls ? Julian. Yes, my own child —
To keep them warm till it begin again. Lily. Is it dark down there ?
[Clinging to JULIAN, and pointing down. Julian. Yes, it is dark; but pleasant—oh, so
sweet !
For out of there come all the pretty flowers. Lily. Did the church grow out of there, with
the
long stalk
That tries to touch the little frightened clouds ? Julian. It did, my darling. —There's a
door
down there That leads away to where the church is pointing.
[She is silent for some time, and keeps looking first down and then up. JULIAN carries

Jier away in his amis.

SCENE XX.— Portsmouth. LORD SEAFORD, partially recovered. Enter LADY GERTRUDE and BERNARD.

Lady Gertrude. I have found an old friend,
father. Here he is ! Lord S. Bernard ! Who would have thought
to see you here !

Bern* I came on Lady Gertrude in the street. I know not which of us was more surprised.
[LADY GERTRUDE goes.

Bern. Where is the countess ?

Lord S. Countess ! What
do you mean ? I do not know.

Bern. The Italian lady.

Lord S. Countess
Lamballa, do you mean ? You frighten me !

Bern. I am glad indeed to know your ignorance; For since I saw the count, I would not have you
Wrong one gray hair upon his noble head.
[LORD SEAFORD covers his eyes -with his hands.

You have not then heard the news about yourself ? Such interesting morsels reach the last A man's own ear. The public has decreed You and the countess run away together. 'Tis certain she has balked the London Argos, And that she has been often to your house. The count believes it—clearly from his face : The man is dying slowly on his feet.

Lord S. (starting up and ringing the bell). O God! what am I ? My love bums like hate, Scorching and blasting with a fiery breath !

Bern. What the deuce ails you, Seaford ? Are you raving ?

Enter Waiter.

. Lord S. Post-chaise for London—four horses— instantly. [He sinks exhausted in his chair.

SCENE XXI.— LILY in ted. JULIAN seated by her.

Lily. O father, take me on your knee, and nurse
me. Another story is very nearly done.
[He takes her on his knees. I am so tired ! Think I should like to go Down to the warm place that the flowers come
from,
Where all the little boys and girls are lying In little beds—white curtains, and white tassels. —No, no, no—it is so dark down there ! Father will not come near me all the night.
Julian. You shall not go, my darling; I will
keep you.

Lily. O will you keep me always, father dear ? And though I sleep ever so sound, still keep me ? I should be so happy, never to move ! 'Tis such a dear well place, here in your arms !
Don't let it take me ; do not let me go : I cannot leave you, father—love hurts so.

Julian. Yes, darling; love does hurt. It is too
good
Never to hurt. Shall I walk with you now, And try to make you sleep ? Lily. Yes—no; for 1 should leave you then.
Oh, my head! Mother, mother, dear mother !—Sing to me,

father.

[He tries to sing.

Oh the hurt, the hurt, and the hurt of love ! Wherever the sun shines, the waters go. It hurts the snowdrop, it hurts the dove, God on his throne, and man below.

But sun would not shine, nor waters go, Snowdrop tremble, nor fair dove moan, God be on high, nor man below, But for love—for the love with its hurt alone

Thou knowest, O Saviour, its hurt and its sorrows, Didst rescue its joy by the might of thy pain :

Lord of all yesterdays, days, and to-morrows Help us love on in the hope of thy gain;

Hurt as it may, love on, love for ever ; Love for love's sake, like the Father above, But for whose brave-hearted Son we had never Known the sweet hurt of the sorrowful love.

[She sleeps at last. He sits as before, ivith the child leaning on his bosom, and falls into a kind of stupor, in which he talks.

Julian. A voice comes from the vacant, wide

sea-vault:

Man with the heart, praying for woman's love, Receive thy prayer : be loved ; and take thy choice: Take this or this. O Heaven and Earth ! I see— What is it ? Statue trembling into life With the first rosy flush upon the skin ? Or woman-ange 1 . richer by lack of wings ? I see her—where I know not; for I see Nought else: she filleth space, and eyes, and

brain—
God keep me !—in celestial nakedness.
She leaneth forward, looking down in space,
With large eyes full of longing, made intense
By mingled fear of something yet unknown;
Her arms thrown forward, circling half; her hands
Half lifted, and half circling, like her arms.
O heavenly artist! whither hast thou gone
To find my own ideal womanhood—
Glory grown grace, divine to human grown ?

I hear the voice again : Speak but the word: She will array herself and come to thee. Lo, at her white foot lie her solar clothes, Her earthly dress for work and weary rest. I see a woman-form, laid as in sleep, Close by the white foot of the wonderful. It is the same shape, line for line, as she. Green grass and daisies shadow round her limbs.

Why speak I not the word ? Clothe thee, and
come,
0 infinite woman ! my life faints for thee.
Once more the voice : Stay I look on this side first:

1 spake of choice. Look here, O son of man ! Choose then between them. Ah ! ah !
[Silence.

Her I knew

Some ages gone ; the woman who did sail Down a long river with me to the sea j Who gave her lips up freely to my lips, Her body willingly into my arms ; Came down from off her statue-pedestal, And was a woman in a common house, Not beautified by fancy every day, And losing worship by her gifts to me. She gave me that white child—what came of her 1 I have forgot. —I opened her great heart, And filled it half-way to the brim with love— With love half wine, half vinegar and gall— And so—and so—she—went away and died ?

0 God ! what was it ?—something terrible—

1 will not stay to choose, nor look again Upon the beautiful. Give me my wife, The woman of the old time on the earth.

0 lovely spirit, fold not thy parted hands, Nor let thy hair weep like a sunset-rain

From thy bent brows, shadowing thy snowy breasts! If thou descend to earth, and find no man To love thee purely, strongly, in his will, Even as he loves the truth, because he will, And when he cannot see it beautiful— Then thou mayst weep, and I will help thee weep. Voice, speak again, and tell my wife to come. 'Tis she, 'tis she, low-kneeling at my feet! In the same dress, same flowing of the hair, As long ago, on earth : is her face changed ? Sweet, my love rains on thee, like a warm shower; My dove descending rests upon thy head ;

bless and sanctify thee for my own :

Lift up thy face, and let me look on thee. Heavens, what a face 1 'Tis hers! It is not hers !

She rises—turns it up from me to God, With great rapt orbs, and such a brow !—the stars Might find new orbits there, and be content. O blessed lips, so sweetly closed that sure Their opening must be prophecy or song ! A high-entranced maiden, ever pure, And thronged with burning thoughts of God an<

Truth !

Vanish her garments ; vanishes the silk That the worm spun, the linen of the flax— O heavens ! she standeth there, my statue-form, With the rich golden torrent-hair, white feet, And hands with rosy palms—my ow i ideal! The woman of my world, with deej if eyes Than I had power to think—and j et my Lilia, My wife, with homely airs of ear' /i about her;

R 2

And dearer to my heart as my lost wife, Than to my soul as its new-found ideal! O, Lilia ! teach me ; at thy knees I kneel; Make me thy scholar j speak, and I will hear.

Yea, all eternity

[He is roused by a cry from the child.

Lily. O, father! put your arms close round

about me.

Kiss me. Kiss me harder, father dear. Now ! I am better now.

[She looks long and passionately in his face. Her eyes close; her head drops backward. She is dead,

SCENE XXII.— A cottage-room. LILIA folding a letter.

Lilia. Now I have told him all; no word kept

back

To burn within me like an evil fire. And where I am, I have told him ; and I wait To know his will. What though he love me not,

If I love him !—I will go back to him,

And wait on him submissive. 'Tis enough

For one life, to be servant to that man !

It was but pride—at best, love stained with pride,

That drove me from him. He and my sweet child

Must miss my hands, if not my eyes and heart.

How lonely is my Lily all the day,

Till he comes home and makes her paradise !

I go to be his servant. Every word That comes from him softer than a command, I'll count it gain, and lay it in my heart, And serve him better for it.—He will receive me.

SCENE XXIII.— LILY lying dead. JULIAN lending over her.

Julian. The light of setting suns be on thee,

child !

Nay, nay, my child ! the light of rising suns Is on thee. Joy is with thee—God is Joy :

Peace to himself, and unto us deep joy ; Joy to himself, in the reflex of our joy. Love be with thee ! yea God, for he is Love. Thou wilt need love, even God's, to give thee joy. Children, they say, are born into a world Where grief is their first portion : thou, I think, Never hadst much of grief—thy second birth Into the spirit-world has taught thee grief, If, orphaned now, thou know'st thy mother's story, And know'st thy father's hardness. O my God, Let not my Lily turn away from me.

Now I am free to follow and find her. Thy truer Father took thee home to him, That he might grant my prayer, and save my wife. I thank him for his gift of thee ; for all That thou hast taught me, blessed little child. I love thee, dear, with an eternal love. And now farewell!
_Kissingher

—no, not farewell; I come.

Years keep not back, they lead me on to thee. Yes, they will also lead me on to her.

Enter a Jew.

Jeiu. What is your pleasure with me ? Here I

am, sir. Julian. Walk into the next room ; then look at

this,

And tell me what you'll give for everything.

[Jew goes.

My darling's death has made me almost happy. Now, now I follow, follow. I'm young again. When I have laid my little one to rest, Among the flowers in that same sunny spot, Straight from her grave I'll take my pilgrim-way ; And, calling up all old forgotten skill, Lapsed social claims, and knowledge of mankind, I'll be a man once more in the loud world. Revived experience in its winding ways, Senses and wits made sharp by sleepless lo 1 ? .

If all the world were sworn to secrecy,

Will guide me to her, sure as questing Death.

I'll follow my wife, follow until I die.

V

How shall I face the Shepherd of the sheep, Without the one ewe-lamb he gave to me ? How find her in great Hades if not here, In this poor little round O of a world ? I'll follow my wife, follow until I find.

Re-enter Jew.

Well, how much ? Name your sum. Be liberal. Jeiv. Let me see this room, too. The things are all Old-fashioned and ill-kept. They're worth but

little. Julian. Say what you will—only make haste

and go.

Jev). Say twenty pounds ? Julian. Well, fetch the money at once,

And take possession. But make haste, I pray.

SCENE XXIV.— The country-churchyard. JULIAN standing by Lily's new-filled grave. He looks very worn and ill.

Julian. Now I can leave thee safely to thy

sleep;

Thou wilt not wake and miss me, my fair child ! Nor will they, for she's fair, steal this ewe-lamb, Out of this fold, while I am gone to seek And find the wandering mother of my lamb. I cannot weep ; I know thee with me still. Thou dost not find it very dark down there ? Would I could go to thee ; I long to go ; My limbs are tired ; my eyes are sleepy too j And fain my heart would cease this beat, beat,

beat.

O gladly would I come to thee, my child, And lay my head upon thy little heart, And sleep in the divine munificence Of thy great love ! But my night has not corre :

She is not rescued yet; and I must go.

\'7bHe turns, but sinks on tJte grave. Recovering and rising.

Now for the world—that's Italy, and her.

SCENE XXV.— The empty room, formerly Lilians. Enter JULIAN.

Julian. How am I here ? Alas ! I do not

know.

[should have been at sea.—Ah, now I know ! I have come here to die. [Lies down on the floor.

Where's Lilia?

I cannot find her. She is here, I know. But O these endless passages and stairs, And dreadful shafts of darkness ! Lilia ! Lilia ! wait for me, child ; I'm coining fast, But something holds me. Let me go, devil! My Lilia, have faith ; they cannot hurt you. You are God's child— they dare not touch you,

wife.

0 pardon me, my beautiful, my own ! [Sings

Wind, wind, thou blowest many a drifting thing From sheltering cove, down to the unsheltered sea ; Thou blowest to the sea my blue sail's wing — Us to a new, love-lit futurity :

Out to the ocean fleet and float—

Blow, blow my little leaf-like boat.

[White he sings, enter LORD SEAFORD, pale and haggard. JULIAN descries him suddenly.

What are you, man ? O brother, bury me— There's money in my pocket

Emptying the Jew's gold on the floor by my child

Staring at him.

Oh! you are Death. Go, saddle the pale horse

1 will not walk — I'll ride. What, skeleton ! cannot sit him ! ha ! ha ! Hither, brute ! Here, Lilia, do the lady's task, my child, And buckle on my spurs. I'll send him up

With a gleam through the blue, snorting white

foam-flakes.

Ah me ! I have not won my golden spurs, Nor is there any maid to bind them on: I will not ride the horse, I'll walk with thee. Come, Death, give me thine arm, poor slave!

—we'll go. Lord Seaford (stooping over kirn). I am Seaford,

Count.

Julian. Seaford! What Seaford ? \'7bRecollecting. — Seaford I \'7bSpringing to his feet. Where is my wife ?

\'7blie falls into SEAFORD'S anns. He lays him down.

Lord S. Had I seen him, she had been safe for me. \'7bGoes.

[JULIAN lies motionless. Insensibility passes into sleep. He -wakes calm, in the sultry dusk of a summer evening.

Julian. Still, still alive ! I thought that I was
dead.

I had a frightful dream ! 'Tis gone, thank God !

He is quiet a little.

So then Thou didst not take the child away That I might find my wife ! Thy will be done. Thou wilt not let me go. This last desire I send away with grief, but willingly. I have prayed to thee, and thou hast heard my

prayer :

Take thou thine own way, only lead her home. Cleanse her, O Lord. I cannot know thy might : But thou art mighty, with a power unlike All, all that we know by the name of power, Transcending it as intellect transcends The stone upon the ground — it may be more , For these are both created—thou creator, Lonely, supreme.

Now it is almost over,

My spirit's journey through this strange sad

world;

This part is done, whatever cometh next. Morning and evening have made out their day ; My sun is going down in stormy dark, But I will face it fearless.

The first act

Is over of the drama.—Is it so ? What means the dim dawn of half-memories Of something I knew once and know not now— Of something differing from all this earth ? I cannot tell; I care not—only know That God will keep the living thing he made. How mighty must he be to have the right Of swaying this great power I feel I am, Moulding and forming it, as pleaseth him ! O God, I come to thee, thou art my life j O God, thou art my home, I come to thee. Can this be death ? Lo 1 I am lifted up

Large-eyed into the night. Nothing I see But that which «•, the living awful Truth ; All forms of which are but the sparks flung out From the luminous ocean clothing round the sun, Himself all dark. Ah ! I remember me : Christ said to Martha—"Whosoever liveth, And doth believe in me, shall never die." I wait, I wait, expecting, till the door Of God's wide theatre be open flung To let me in. What wonders I shall see ! The expectation fills me, like new life Dancing through all my veins.

Once more I thank thee For all that thou hast made me—most of all, That thou didst make me wander and seek thee. I thank thee for my wife : to thee I trust her ; Forget her not, my God. If thou save her, I shall be able then to thank thee so As will content thee—with full-flowing song,

The very bubbles on whose dancing waves Are daring thoughts flung faithful at thy feet.

My heart sinks in me—I grow faint. Oh! whence This wind of love that fans me out of life ? One stoops to kiss me—Ah, my lily child ! God hath not flung thee over his garden-wall.

[Re-enter LORD SEAFORD with the doctor. JULIAN takes no heed of them. te doctor shakes his head.

My little child, I'll never leave thee more ; We are both children now in God's big house. Come, lead me; you are older here than I By three whole days, my darling angel-child !

[A letter is brought in. LORD SEAFORD holds it before JULIAN'S eyes. He looks vaguely at it.

Lord S. It is a letter from your wife, I think. Julian (feebly]. A letter from my Lilia ! Bury it with me— I'll read it in my chamber, by and by:

Dear words should not be read with others nigh. Lilia, my wife ! I am going home to God. Lord S. (bending over hint). I'll pledge my soul your wife is innocent.

[JULIAN gazes at him blankly. A light begins to grow in his eyes. It grows till his face is transfigured. It vanishes. He dies.

END OF PART IV.

TOL. r.

WITHIN AND WITHOUT.

PART V.

AND do not fear to hope. Can poet's brain
More than the father's heart rich good invent ?
Each time we smell the autumn's dying scent,
We know the primrose time will come again ;
Not more we hope, nor less would soothe our pain.
Be bounteous in thy faith, for not mis-spent
Is confidence unto the Father lent:
Thy need is sown and rooted for his rain.
His thoughts are as thine own ; nor are his ways
Other than thine, but by their loftier sense
Of beauty infinite and love intense.
Work on. One day, beyond all thoughts of praise,
A sunny joy will crown thee with its rays ;
Nor other than thy need, thy recompense.

S 2

PART V.

A DREAM. SCENE I. "A world not realized." LILY. To her, JULIAN.

Lily. O father, come with me ! I have founa her—mother.

SCENE II.— A room in a cottage. LILIA on her knees before a. crucifix. Her back only is seen, for tlte Poet dares not look on her face. On a chair beside her lies a book, open at CHAPTER VIII. Behind her stands an Angel, bending forward, as if to protect her with his wings partly expanded. Appear JULIAN, with LILY in his arms. LILY looks with love on the angel, and a kind of longing fear on her mother.

Julian. Angel, thy part is done; leave her to me. Angel. Sorrowful man, to thee I must give place j

Thy ministry is stronger far than mine ; Yet have I done my part.—She sat with him. He gave her rich white flowers with crimson scent, The tuberose and datura ever burning Their incense to the dusky face of night. He spoke to her pure words of lofty sense, But tinged with poison for a tranced ear. He bade low music sound of faint farewells, Which fixed her eyes upon a leafy picture, Wherein she wandered through an amber twilight Towards a still grave in a sleepy nook. And ever and anon she sipped pale wine, Rose-tinged, rose-odoured, from a silver cup. He sang a song, each pause of which closed up, Like a day-wearied daisy for the night, With these words falling like an echo low : " Love, let us love and weep and faint and die." With the last pause the tears flowed at their will, Without a sob, down from their cloudy gUies.

SCENE ii. WITHIN AND WITHOUT.

He took her hand in his, and it ky still.—

A blast of music from a wandering band

Billowed the air with sudden storm that moment.
The visible rampart of material things
Was rent—the vast eternal void looked in
Upon her awe-struck soul. She cried and fled.
It was the sealing of her destiny.
A wild convulsion shook her inner world
Its lowest depths were heaved turnultuously
Far unknown molten gulfs of being rushed
Up into mountain-peaks, rushed and remained.
The soul that led a fairy life, athirst
For beauty only, passed into a woman's :
In pain and tears was born the child-like need
For God, for Truth, and for essential Love.
But first she woke in terror; was alone,
For God she saw not j—woke up in the night,
The great wide night. No mother's hand had she
To soothe her pangs, no father's voice to cheer.
She would not come to thee ; for love itself
Too keenly stung her sad, repentant heart,
Giving her bitter names to name herself;
But calling back old words which thou liadst
spoken
In other days, by light winds borne away, Returning in the storm of wretchedness, Hither she came to seek her Julian's God. So now farewell! My care of her is over. Julian. A heart that knows what thou canst
never know,
Fair angel, blesseth thee, and saith, farewell.
[The Angel goes. JULIAN and LILY take his place. LILIA is praying, and they hear parts of her prayer.
Lilia. O Jesus, hear me! Let me speak to thee. No fear oppresses me ; for misery Fills my heart up too full for any fear.
Is there no help, O Holy ? Am I stained Beyond release ?
Julian. Lilia, thy purity
Maketh thy heart abuse thee. I, thy husband, Sinned more against thee, in believing ill, Than thou, by ten times what thou didst, poor
child, Hadst wronged thy husband.
Lilia. Pardon will not do :
I need much more, O Master. That word go Surely thou didst not speak to send away The sinful wife thou wouldst not yet condemn ! Or was that crime, though not too great for
pardon,
Too great for loving-kindness afterwards ? Certain, she came again behind thy feet, And weeping, wiped, and kissed them, Mary's
son!
Blessed for ever with a heavenly grief. Ah ! she nor I can claim with her who gave The best she had, her tears, her hair, her lips,

WITHIN AND WITHOUT. PART v

To soothe feet hard with Galilean roads :— She sinned against herself, not against—Julian.

O God, O God, find some excuse for me. Wilt thou not find something to say for me, As for the crowd that cried against thee, then, When heaven was dark, because thy lamp burned low?

Julian. Not thou, but I am guilty, Lilta. I made it possible to tempt thee, child. Thou didst not fall, beloved ; only, one moment Beauty was queen, and Truth not lord of all.

Lilia. O Julian, my husband—it is strange— But when I think of Him, he looks like thee ; And when he speaks to comfort me, the voice Is like thy voice, my husband, my beloved ! Oh ! if I could but lie down at thy feet, And tell thee all, yes, every word, I know That thou wouldst think the best that could be thought,

SCENE ii. WITHIN AND WITHOUT

And love and comfort me. O Julian, I am more thine than ever. Forgive me, husband, For calling me, denied and outcast, thine. Yet may I not be thine as I am .His ? Would I might be thy servant—yes, thy slave, To wash thy feet, and dress thy lovely child, And bring her at thy call—more wife than I. But I shall never see thee, till the earth Lies on us both—apart—oh, far apart! How lonely shall I lie the long, long years ! Lily. O mother, there are blue skies here, and

flowers,

And blowing winds, and kisses, mother dear. And every time my father kisses me, It is not father only, but Another. Make haste and come. My head never aches

here. Lilia. Can it be that they are dead ? Is it

possible ?

I feel as if they were near me !—Speak again, Beloved voices ! comfort me ; I need it.
Julian (singing).
Come to us ; above the storm
Ever shines the blue. Come to us : beyond its form
Ever lies the True.
Lily (singing).
Mother, darling, do not weep—
All I cannot tell: By and by, you'll go to sleep,
And you'll wake so well.
Julian (singing).
There is sunshine everywhere
For thy heart and mine : God, for every sin and care,
Is the cure divine.
Lily (singing).
We're so happy all the day,
Waiting for another: All the flowers and sunshine stay,
Waiting for you, mother.
»CEWE in. WITHIN AND WITHOUT.
Julian. My maiden! for true wife is maiden
ever
To the true husband : them art mine for ever. Lilia. What gentle hopes are passing to and fro! Thou shadowest me with thine own rest, my
God; A cloud from thee stoops down and covers me.
[Shefalls asleep on her knees.

SCENE III.— JULIAN on the summit of a mountain-peak. The stars are brilliant around a crescent moon, hanging half-way between the mountain and the sky. Below lies a sea of vapour. Beyond rises a loftier pinnacle, across which is stretched a bar of cloud. LILY lies on the cloud, looking earnestly into the mist below.

Julian (gazing upwards). And thou wert with
me all the time, my God, Even as now ! I was not far from thee. Thy spirit spoke in all my wants and fears, And hopes and longings. Thou art all Va all.

I am not mine, but thine. I cannot speak The thoughts that work within me like a sea. When on the earth I lay, crushed down beneath The hopeless weight of empty desolation, Thy sympathizing face was lighted then With expectation of my joy to come, When all the realm of possible ill should lie Under my feet, and I should stand as now All-sure of thee, true-hearted, only One. Was ever heart filled to such overflowing With the pure wine of blessedness, my God ? Filled as the night with stars, am I with joys; Filled as the heavens with thee, am I with

peace;
For now I wait the end of all my prayers, Of all that have to do with old-world things : What new things come to wake new prayers, my

God, Thou knowest, and I wait in perfect peace.
He turns his gaze downwards. — Front the fog-sea below Jtalf-rises a woman-form, which floats towards him

Lo, as the lily lifts its shining bosom Above the couch of waters where it slept, When the bright morn toucheth and waketh it; So riseth up my lily from the deep Where human souls are tried in awful dreams.

[LiLY spies her mother, darts down into the fog, and is caught in her arms. They land on JULIAN'S peak, and climb, LILY leading her

mother.
Lily. Come faster, mother dear j father is waiting. Lilia. Have patience with me, darling. By and

by,
think I shall do better.—O my Julian ! Julian. I may not help her. She must climb and come.

\'7bHe reaches his hand, and the three are clasped m an infinite embrace.
O God, thy thoughts, thy ways, are not as
ours: They fill our longing hearts up to the brim.

[The moon and the stars and the bine night clatt around them; and the Poet awakes frem ku> dream.

THE END-

A HIDDEN LIFE.

TO
MY FATHER.

TAKE of the first fruits, Father, of thy care, Wrapped in the fresh leaves of my gratitude,
L.ate waked for early gifts ill understood ;

Claiming in all my harvests rightful share,

Whether with song that mounts the joyful air I praise my God, or, in yet deeper mood, Sit
dumb because I know a speechless good,

Needing no voice, but all the soul for prayer. Thou hast been faithful to my highest need ;

And I, thy debtor, ever, evermore,

Shall never feel the grateful burden sore. Yet most I thank thee, not for any deed, But for
the sense thy living self did breed

That fatherhood is at the great world's core.

T 3

TO MY FA THER.

All childhood, reverence clothed thee, undefined,

As for some being of another race ;

Ah ! not with it, departing — grown apace, As years have brought me manhood's loftier
mind Able to see thy human life behind —

The same hid heart, the same revealing face —

My own dim contest settling into grace Of sorrow, strife, and victory combined.

So I beheld my God, in childhood's morn, A mist, a darkness, great, and far apart,
Moveless and dim — I scarce could say Thou art

My manhood came, of joy and sadness born —

Full soon the misty dark, asunder torn, Revealed man's glory, God's great human heart.

G. M. D.Jr.

Algiers, April, 1857.

A HIDDEN LIFE.

ROUDLY the youth, sudden with manhood crowned,

Went walking by his horses, the first time

That morning, to the plough. No soldier gay Feels at his side the throb of the gold hilt
(Knowing the blue blade hides within its sheath, As lightning in the cloud) with more delight,
When first he belts it on, than he that day Heard still the clank of the plough-chains against The
horses' harnessed sides, as to the field They went to make it fruitful. O'er the hill The sun looked
down, baptizing him for toil

A HIDDEN LIFE.

A farmer's son, a farmer's grandson he ; Yea, his great-grandsire had possessed those
fields. Tradition said they had been tilled by men Who bore the name long centuries ago, And
married wives, and reared a stalwart race, And died, and went where all had followed them, Save
one old man, his daughter, and the youth Who ploughs in pride, nor ever doubts his toil; And
death is far from him this sunny morn. Why should we think of death when life is high ? The
earth laughs all the day, and sleeps all night. The daylight's labour and the night's repose Are
very good, each better in its time.

The boy knew little ; but he read old tales Of Scotland's warriors, till his blood ran swift

As charging knights upon their death career. He chanted ancient tunes, till the wild blood Was charmed back into its fountain-well, And tears arose instead. That poet's songs,

Whose music evermore recalls his name, His name of waters babbling as they run. Rose from him in the fields among the kine, And met the sky-lark's, raining from the clouds. But only as the birds he sang as yet, From rooted impulse of essential =ong ; The earth was fair—he knew not it was faL • His heart was glad—he knew not it was gla He walked as in a twilight of the sense, Which this one day shall turn to tender light

Long ere the sun had cleared the feathery topi Of the fir-thicket on the eastward hill, His horses leaned and laboured. Each great hand Held rein and plough-stilt in one guiding grasp— No ploughman there would brook a helper. Proud With a time ploughman's pride—nobler, I think, Than statesman's, ay, or poet's, painter's pride, For little praise will come that he ploughs well — He did plough well, proud of his work itself,

And not of what would follow. With sure eye. He saw his horses keep the arrow-track; He saw the swift share cut the measured sod; He saw the furrow folding to the right, Ready with nimble foot to aid at need : Turning its secrets upward to the sun, And hiding in the dark the sun-born grass, And daisies dipped in carmine, lay the tilth— A million graves to nurse the buried grain, And send a golden harvest up the air.

When the steep sun had clomb to his decline, And pausing seemed, at edge of slow descent, Upon the keystone of his airy bridge, They rested likewise, half-tired man and horse, And homeward went for food and courage new. Therewith refreshed, they turned again to toil, And lived in labour all the afternoon ; Till, in the gloaming, once again the plough Lay like a stranded bark upon the lea,

And home with hanging neck the horses went, Walking beside their master, force by will. Then through the lengthening shadows came a show.

It was a lady mounted on a horse, A slender girl upon a mighty steed, That bore her with the pride horses must feel When they submit to women. Home she went, Alone, or else her groom lagged far behind. Scarce had she bent simple acknowledgment Of the hand in silent salutation lifted To the bowed head, when something faithless

yielded,

The saddle slipped, the horse stopped, and the girl Stood on her feet, still holding fast the reins.

Three paces bore him bounding to her side ; Her radiant beauty almost fixed him there ; But with main force, as one that grapples fear, He threw the fascination off, and saw

The work before him. Soon his hand and knife Had set the saddle firmer than before Upon the gentle horse ; and then he turned To mount the maiden. But bewilderment A moment lasted ; for he knew not how, With stirrup-hand and steady arm, to throne, Elastic, on her steed, the ascending maid : A moment only; for while yet she thanked, Nor yet had time to teach her further will, About her waist he put his brawny hands, That all but zoned her round ; and like a child Lifting her high, he set her on the horse ; Whence like a risen moon she smiled on him, Nor turned aside, although a radiant blush Shone in her cheek, and shadowed in her eyes. But he was never sure if from her heart Or from the rosy sunset came the flush. Again she thanked him, while again he stood Bewildered in her beauty. Not a word

Answered her words that flowed, folded in tones

Round which dissolving lambent music played,
Like dropping water in a silver cup ;
Till, round the shoulder of the neighbouring hill,
Sudden she disappeared. And he awoke,
And called himself hard names, and turned and
went After his horses, bending too his head.

Ah God ! when Beauty passes from the door, Although she came not in, the house is bare : Shut, shut the door ; there's nothing in the house. Why seems it always that she should be ours ? A secret lies behind which thou dost know, And I can partly guess.

But think not then,
The holder of the plough sighed many sighs Upon his bed that night; or other dreams Than pleasant rose upon his view in sleep ; Nor think the aiiy castles of his brain

Had less foundation than the air admits. But read my simple tale, scarce worth the name ; And answer, if he had not from the fair Beauty's best gift; and proved her not, in sooth, An angel vision from a higher world.

Not much of her I tell. Her glittering life, Where part the waters on the mountain-ridge, Ran down the southern side, apart from his, Yet was not over-blessed ; for, I know, Her tale wiled many sighs, one summer eve, From him who in the mysteries of a wood Walking, received it from beloved lips. But now she was as God had made her, ere The world had tried to spoil her ; tried, I say, And half-succeeded, failing utterly. Fair was she, frank, and innocent as a child That stares in every eye ; fearless of ill, 2«rause she knew it not; and brave withal, Because she led a simple country life,

Much in the open air. Her father's house— A Scottish laird was he, of ancient name — Was but two miles away among the hills ; Yet often as she passed his father's farm, The youth had never seen her face before, And should not twice. Yet was it not enough ? The vision tarried. She, as the harvest moon That goeth on her way, and knoweth not The fields of corn whose ripening grain she fills With strength of life, and Hope, and joy for men, Went on her way, and knew not of the virtue Gone out of her; yea, never thought of him, Save at such times as, all at once, old scenes Return uncalled, with wonder that they come. Soon was she orphaned of her parent-haunts, And rounded with dead glitter, not the shine Of leaves and waters dancing in the sun y But he abode in ever-breaking dawns, Breathed ever new-born winds into his soul;

And saw the aurora of a greater dawn Climbing the hill-sides of the heapy world.

Again I say, no fond romance of love, No argument of possibilities, If he were some one, and she sought his help, Turned his clear brain into a nest of dreams. As soon he had sat down and twisted cords To snare, and carry home for daylight aid, Some woman-angel, wandering half-seen On moonlight wings, o'er withered autumn fields. But when he rose next mom, and went abroad, (The exultation of his new-found rank Already settling into dignity,) He found the earth was beautiful. The sky Shone with the expectation of the sun. He grieved him for the daisies, for they fell Caught in the furrow, with their innocent heads Just out imploring. A gray hedgehog ran With tangled mesh of bristling spikes, and face

Helplessly innocent, across the field : He let it run, and blessed it as it ran. Returned at noon-tide, something drew his feet Into the barn : entering, he gazed and stood. For, through the rent roof lighting, one sunbeam Blazed on the yellow straw one golden spot, Dulled all the amber heap, and sinking far, Like flame inverted, through the loose-piled
mound,
Crossed the keen splendour with dark shadow-straws,

In lines innumerable. 'Twas so bright, His eye was cheated with a spectral smoke That rose as from a fire. He had not known How beautiful the sunlight was, not even Upon the windy fields of morning grass, Nor on the river, nor the ripening corn. As if to catch a wild live thing, he crept On tiptoe silent, laid him on the heap,

And gazing down into the glory-gulf, Dreamed as a boy half-sleeping by the fire; And dreaming rose, and got his horses out.

God, and not woman, is the heart of all. But she, as priestess of the visible earth, Holding the key, herself most beautiful, Had come to him, and flung the portals wide. He entered in : each beauty was a glass That gleamed the woman back upon his view. Shall I not rather say : each beauty gave Its own soul up to him who worshipped her, For that his eyes were opened thus to see ?

Already in these hours his quickened soul Put forth the white tip of a floral bud, Ere long to be a crown-like, aureole flower. His songs unbidden, his joy in ancient tales, Had hitherto alone betrayed the seed That lay in his heart, close hidden even from him, Yet not the less mellowing all his spring :

A HIDDEN LIFE.

Like summer sunshine came the maiden's face,
And in the youth's glad heart, the seed awoke.
It grew and spread, and put forth many flowers,
And every flower a living open eye,
Until his soul was full of eyes within.
Each morning now was a fresh boon to him ;
Each wind a spiritual power upon his life ;
Each individual animal did share
A common being with him ; every kind
Of flower from every other was distinct,
Uttering that for which alone it was—
Its something human, wrapt in other veil.

And when the winter came, when thick the snow Armed the sad fields from gnawing of the frost, When the low sun but skirted his far realms, And sank in early nigh f , he drew his chair Beside the fire ; and by the feeble lamp Read book on book; and wandered other climes, And lived in other lives and other needs,

VOL I. U

ago A HIDDEN LIFE.

And grew a larger self by other selves
Ere long, the love of knowledge had become
A hungry passion and a conscious power,
And craved for more than reading could supply.
Then, through the night (all dark, except the moon
Shone frosty o'er the heath, or the white snow
Gave back such motes of light as else had sunk
"Si the dark earth) he bent his plodding way
Over the moors to where the little town
Lay gathered in the hollow. There the student
Who taught from lingering dawn to early dark,
Had older scholars in the long fore-night;

For youths who in the shop, or in the barn,
Or at the loom, had done their needful work,
Came gathering through starlight, fog, or snow,
And found the fire ablaze, the candles lit,
And him who knew waiting for who would know.
Here mathematics wiled him to their heights ;
And strange consent of lines to form and law

Made Euclid a profound romance of truth. The master saw with wonder that the youth So eagerly devoured the offered food, And longed to lead him further; for fair knowledge Would multiply like life; and two clear souls That see one truth, and, turning, also see Each other's face glow in that truth's delight, Are something more than lovers. So he offered To guide him through the narrow ways that lead To lofty heights of Roman speech. The youth Caught at the offer ; and for many a night, When others slept, he groped his twilight way With lexicon and rule, through ancient story, Or fable line, embalmed in Latin old ; Wherein his knowledge of the English tongue (Through reading many books) much aided him™' For the best is alike in every tongue.

At length his progress, through the master's word,

u 2

Proud of such pupil, reached the father's ears. Great gladness woke within him, and he vowed, If caring, sparing might accomplish it, He should to college, and should have his fill Of that same learning.

To the plough no more, All day to school he went; and ere a year, He wore the scai'let gown with the closed sleeves.

Awkward at first, but with a dignity Soon finding fit embodiment in speech And gesture and address, he made his way, Not seeking such, to the full-orbed respect Of students and professors ; for whose praise More than his worth, society, so called, To its rooms in that great city of the North, Invited him. He entered. Dazzled at first By brilliance of the outer show, the lights, The mirrors, gems, white necks, and radiant eyes, He stole into a corner, and was quiet

Until the vision too had quieter grown. Bewildered next by many a sparkling word, Nor knowing the light-play of polished minds, Which, like rose-diamonds cut in many facets, Catch and reflect the wandering rays of truth As if they were home-born and issuing new, He held his peace, and, silent soon began To see how little fire it needs to shine. Hence, in the midst of talk, his thoughts would

wander

Back to the calm divine of homely toil; And round him still and ever hung an air Of breezy fields, and plough, and cart, and scythe— A kind of clumsy grace, in which gay girls Saw but the clumsiness—another sort Saw the grace too, yea, sometimes, when he spoke, Saw the grace only ; and began at last, For he sought none, to seek him in the crowd, And find him unexpected, maiden-wise.

But oftener far they sought than found him

thus,

For seldom was he drawn away from toil. Seldomer yet he stinted toil's due time ; For if one eve his panes were dark, the next They gleamed far into morning. And he won Honours among the first, each session's close.

Nor think that new familiarity With open forms of ill, not to be shunned Where many youths are met, endangered much A mind that had begun to will the pure. Oft when the broad rich humour of a jest With breezy force drew in its skirts a troop Of pestilential vapours

following— Arose within his sudden silent mind, The maiden face that once blushed down on
him,
That lady face, insphered beyond his earth, Yet visible as bright, particular star.
A flush of tenderness then glowed across
His bosom—shone it clean from passing harm.
Should that sweet face be banished by rude
words ?
It could not stay what maidens might not hear. He almost wept for shame, that face, that
jest Should meet in his house : to his love he made Love's only worthy offering—purity.

And if the homage that he sometimes met, New to the country lad, conveyed in smiles,
Assents, and silent listenings when he spoke, Threatened yet more his life's simplicity ; An
antidote of nature ever came, Even Nature's self. For, in the summer months, His former haunts
and boyhood's circumstance Received him to the bosom of their grace. 'And he, too noble to
despise the past, Too proud to be ashamed of manly toil, Too wise to fancy that a gulf lay wide
Betwixt the labouring hand and thinking brain, Or that a workman was no gentleman
Because a workman, clothed himself again In his old garments, took the hoe, the spade, The
sowing sheet, or covered in the grain, Smoothing with harrows what the plough had
ridged.
With ever fresher joy he hailed the fields, Returning still with larger powers of sight:
Each time he knew them better than before, And yet their sweetest aspect was the old. His labour
kept him true to life and fact, Casting out worldly judgments, false desires, And vain distinctions.
Ever, at his toil, New thoughts arose; which, when still night
awoke,
He ever sought, like stars, with instruments ; By science, or by wise philosophy, Bridging
the gulf betwixt the new and old.
Thus laboured he with hand and brain at once, Preparing for the time when Scotland's
sons Reap wisdom in the silence of the year.
His sire was proud of him ; and, most of all, Because his learning did not make him
proud. A wise man builds not much upon his lore. The neighbours asked what he would make
his
son.
" I'll make a man of him," the old man said ; " And for the rest, just what he likes himself.
He is my only son—I think he'll keep The old farm on, and I shall go content, Leaving a man
behind me, as I say."
So four years long his life went to and fro, Alternating the red gown and blue coat, The
garret study and the wide-floored bam, The wintry city and the sunny fields. In every change his
mind was well content, For in himself he was the growing same.
Nor iii one channel flowed his seeking thoughts; To no profession did he ardent turn : He
knew his father's wish—it was his own. "Why should a man," he said, "when knowledge
grows,
Leave therefore the old patriarchal life, And seek distinction in the noise of men ? " He
turned his asking face on every side ; Went reverent with the anatomist, and saw The inner form
of man laid skilful bare ; Went with the chymist, whose wise-questioning
hand
Made Nature do in little, before his eyes, And momently, what, huge, for centuries, And
in the vcil of vastness and lone deeps, She labours at; bent his inquiring eye On every source

whence knowledge flows for
men: At some he only sipped, at others drank.
At length, when he had gained the master's
right—

A custom sacred from of old—to sit With covered head before the awful rank Of black-gowned senators ; and each of those, Proud of his pupil, was ready at a word To speed him on towards any further goal; He took his books, his well-worn cap and gown, And, leaving with a sigh the ancient walls, The grand old crown of stone, unchanging gray In all the blandishments of youthful spring, He sought for life the lone ancestral farm.

With simple gladness met him on the road His gray-haired father—elder brother now. Few words were spoken, little welcome said, But on each side the more was understood, If with a less delight he brought him home Than he who met the prodigal returned, It was with more reliance, with more peace \

For with the leaning pride that old men feel
In young strong arms that draw their might from
them,
He led him to the house. His sister there, Whose kisses were not many, but whose eyes Were full of watchfulness and hovering love, Set him beside the fire in the old place, And heaped the table with best country fare.

When the swift night grew deep, the father rose, And led him, wondering why and where they went, Thorough the limpid dark, with tortuous path Between the corn-ricks, to a loft above The stable where the same old horses slept, Which he had guided that eventful morn. Entering he saw some plan-pursuing hand Had ueen at work. The father, leading on Across the floor, heaped high with store of grain. Opened a door. An unexpected light Flashed on him cheerful from a fire and lamp,

That burned alone, as in a fairy tale.
Behold ! a little room, a curtained bed,
An easy chair, bookshelves, and writing desk,
An old print of a deep Virgilian wood,
And one of choosing Hercules ! The youth
Gazed and spoke not. The old paternal love
Had sought and found an incarnation new ;
For, honouring in his son the simple needs
Which his own bounty had begot in him,
He gave him thus a lonely thinking space,
A silent refuge. With a quiet good night,
He left him dumb with love. Faintly beneath.
The horses stamped and drew the lengthening
chain.
Three sliding years, with slowly blended change. Drew round their winter, summer, autumn, spring, Fulfilled of work by hands, and brain, and heart. He laboured as before ; though when he would, And Nature urged not, he, with privilege,
Would spare from hours of toil—read in his room.
Or wander thi ough the moorland to the hills;
There on the apex of the world would stand,
As on an altar, burning, soul and heart,

Himself the sacrifice of faith and prayer ;
Gaze in the face of the inviting blue
That domed him round ; ask why it should be
blue;
Pray yet again ; and with love-strengthened heart Go down to lower things with lofty
cares.
When Sundays came, the father, daughter, son Walked to the church across their own
loved
fields.
It was an ugly church, with scarce a sign Of what makes English churches venerable.
Likest a crowing cock upon a heap It stood—but let us say—St. Peter's cock; For, sure, it lacked
not many a holy charm To whom it was coeval with his being—
Dawning with it from darkness of the unseen. And the low mounds of monumental grass
Were far more solemn than great marble tombs ; For flesh is grass, its goodliness the flower. Oh
lovely is the face of country graves On sunny afternoons ! The light itself Nestles amidst the
grass ; and the sweet wind Says, I am here, —no more. With sun and wind And crowing cocks,
who can believe in death ? He, on such days, when from the church they
came, And through God's ridges took their thoughtful
way,
The last psalm lingering lowly in their hearts, Would look, inquiring where his ridge
would
rise;
But when it gloomed and rained, he turned aside : What mattered it to him ?
And as they walked
Home from the church, the father loved to hear The fresh rills pouring from his son's
clear well. For the old man clung not to the old alone; Nor leaned the young man only to the new
', They would the best, and sought, and followed it. The pastor's lore was sound, his teaching
poor; The Past alone he cherished, said our friend ; Honoured those Jewish times as he were a
Jew, But had no ear for this poor needy hour, Which wanders up and down the centuries, Like
beggar boy roaming the wintry streets, With hand held out to any passer by ; And yet God made
the voice of its many cries. He used to say: "Mine be the work that
comes
First ready to my hand. The lever set I grasp and heave withal. Or let me say, I love
where I live, and let my labour flow Into the hollows of the neighbour-needs.
Perhaps I like it best: I would not choose Another than the ordered circumstance. This
farm is God's as much as yonder town , These men and maidens, kine and horses, his For them
his laws must be incarnated In act and fact, and so their world redeemed." Though thus he spoke
at times, he spoke not
oft;
But ruled by action—what he said he did. No grief was suffered there of man or beast
More than was need ; no creature fled in fear; All slaying was with generous suddenness, Like
God's benignant lightning. " For," he said, " God makes the beasts, and loves them dearly
well—
Better than any parent loves his child, It may be," would he say ; for still the mdy be Was
sacred with him no less than the is — In such humility he lived and wrought—
VOL. I. 1C

" Hence are they sacred. Sprung from God as
we,
They are our brethren in a lower kind; And in their face I see the human look." If any said
: " Men look like animals ; Each has his type set in the lower kind ;" His answer was : " The
animals are like men, Each has his true type set in the higher kind, Though even there only
rough-hewn as yet." He said that cruelty would need no hell Save that the ghosts of the sad
beasts should come, And crowding, silent, all their centred heads, Stare the ill man to madness.
When he spoke,
His word had all the force of unborn deeds That lay within him ready to be born. His
goodness ever went beyond his word, Embodying itself unconsciously In understanding of the
need that prayed,

A HIDDEN LIFE.

And help to which he had not pledged himself; For, like his race, the pledge with him
was slow. When from great cities came the old sad news Of crime and wretchedness, and
children sore With hunger, and neglect, and cruel blows, He would walk sadly all the afternoon,
With head down-bent, and pondering footstep
slow;
Arriving ever at the same result— Concluding ever : " The best that I can do For the great
world, is the same best I can For this my world. What truth may be therein Will pass beyond my
narrow circumstance, In truth's own right." When a philanthropist Said pompously: " It is not for
your gifts To spend themselves on common labours thus : You owe the world far nobler things
than such ;" He answered him: "The world is in God's hands This part in mine, Hither my sacred
past,

X 2

With all its loves inherited, has led, Here left me fit. Shall I judge, arrogant, Primseval,
godlike work in earth and air, Seed time and harvest—offered fellowship With God in nature—
unworthy of my hands ? I know what you would say—I know with grief— The crowds of men,
in whom a starving soul Cries through the windows of their hollow eyes For bare humanity, and
leave to grow :— Would I could help them! But all crowds are
made
Of individuals ; and their grief, and pain, And thirst, and hunger, all are of the one, Not of
the many: the true saving power Enters the individual door, and thence Issues again in thousand
influences Besieging other doors. You cannot throw A. mass of good into the general midst
Whereof each man can seize his private share ;

A HIDDEN LIFE.

Or if you could, it were of lowest kind,
Not reaching to that hunger of the soul.
Now here I labour whole in the same place
Where they have known me from my childhood up,
And I know them, each individual:
If there is power in me to help my own,
Even of itself it flows beyond my will,
Takes shape in commonest of common acts
Meeting the humble day's necessity :
—I would not always consciously do good,
Not always work from full intent of help,

Lest I forget the measure heaped and pressed
And running over which they pour for me ;
And never reap the too-much of return
In smiling trust, and wealth of kindly eyes.
But in the city, with a few lame words
And a few wretched coins, sore-coveted,
To mediate 'twixt my cannot and my would,
My best attempts could hardly strike a root ;

My scattered corn would turn to wind-blown chaft And I grow weak, and weary of my kind, M isunderstood the most where almost known, Baffled and beaten by their unbelief: Years could not place me where I stand this day-High on the vantage-ground of confidence : I might for years toil on, and reach no man. Besides, to leave the thing that nearest lies, And choose the thing far off, more difficult— The act, having no touch of God in it, Who seeks the needy for the pure need's sake, Must straightway die, choked in its selfishness." Thus he. The world-wise schemer for the good Held his poor peace, and went his trackless way.

What of the vision now ? the vision fail-Sent forth to meet him, when at eve he went Home from his first day's ploughing? Oft he

dreamed She passed him smiling on her stately horse;

But never band or buckle yielded more ; Never again his hands enthroned the maid ; He only gazed and worshipped and awoke. Nor woke he then with foolish vain regret; But, saying, " I have seen the beautiful," Smiled with his eyes upon a flower or bird, Or any living form of gentleness That met him first; and all that day, his face Would oftener dawn into a blossomy smile.

And ever when he read a lofty tale, Or when the storied leaf, or ballad old, Or spake or sang of woman very fair, Or wondrous good, he saw her face alone, The genius henceforth of the tale or song.

Nor did he turn aside from other maids, But loved their faces pure and faithful eyes. He may have thought, " One day I wed a maid.. And make her mine ;" but never came the maid, Or never came the hour : he walked alone.

Meantime how fared the lady ? She had wed One of the common crowd. There must be ore For the gold grains to lie in : virgin gold Lies by the dross, enriching not the dross. She was not one who of herself could fo, And she had found no heart, that, one with hers, Would sound accord. She sat alone in the house, And read the last new novel, vaguely, faintly Desiring better; or listlessly conversed With phantom-visitors—they were no friends, But spectral forms from fashion's hollow glass. She haunted gay assemblies, ill-content; But, better there than lonely with her mate, There danced, or sat and talked.

What had she felt,

If through the rhythmic motion of fair forms A vision had arisen—as when, of old, The minstrel's art laid bare the seer's eye, And showed him plenteous waters in the waste—

If the gay dance had vanished from her eyes, And she had seen her ploughman-lover go With his great stride across a lonely field, Under the dark blue vault ablaze with stars, Lifting his full eyes to the radiant roof ? Or in the emerging vision had she seen Him, studious, with space-compelling mind, Bent o'er his slate, pursue some planet's course ; Or read, and justify the poet's wrath, Or sage's slow conclusion ?—If a voice Had whispered then : This man in many a dream And many a moment of keen consciousness, Blesses you for the look that woke his heart, That smiled him into life, and, still unwithered, Lies cherished in the cabinet of his soul— Would those dark eyes have beamed with darkei

light ?

Would that fair soul, half-dead with emptiness, Have risen from the couch of her unrest,
And looked to heaven again, again believed
In God and the realities of life ?
Would not that soul have sung to her lone self:
" I have a friend, a ploughman, who is wise.
He knows what God, and goodness, and fair faith
Mean in the words and books of mighty men.
He little heeds the outer shows of things,
But worships the unconquerable truth.
This man of men loves me : I will be proud
And very humble. If he knew me well,
Would he go on to love me as he loves ? "

In the third year, a heavy harvest fell, Full filled, before the reaping-hook and scythe. The men and maidens in the scorching heat Lightened their toil by merry jest and song ; Rested at mid-day, and from brimming bowl, Drank the brown ale, and white abundant milk ; Until the last ear fell, and stubble stood Where waved the forests of the murmuring corn

And o'er the land rose piled the shocks, like tents
Of an encamping army, tent by tent,
To stand until the moon should have her will.

The grain was ripe. The harvest carts went out Broad-platformed, bearing back the towering load, With frequent passage 'twixt homeyard and field. And half the oats already hid their tops, Their ringing, rustling, wind-responsive sprays, In the still darkness of the towering stack ; When in the north low billowy clouds appeared, Blue-based, white-crested, in the afternoon ; And westward, darker masses, plashed with blue, And outlined vague in misty steep and dell, Clomb o'er the hill-tops : thunder was at hand. The air was sultry. But the upper sky Was clear and radiant.

Downward went the sun, Below the sullen clouds that walled the west, Below the hills, below the rhadowed world.

The moon looked over the clear eastern wall, And slanting rose, and looked, and rose and looked, Searching for silence in her yellow fields. There it was not. For there the staggering carts, Like overladen beasts, crawled homeward still, Returning light and low. The laugh broke yet. That lightning of the soul's unclouded skies, Though not so frequent, now that labour passed Its natural hour. Yet on the labour went, Straining to beat the welkin-climbing toil Of the huge rain-clouds, heavy with their floods. Sleep, old enchantress, sided with the clouds, The crawling clouds, and threw benumbing spells On man and horse. One youth who walked beside A ponderous load of sheaves, higher than wont, Which dared the slumbering leven overhead, Woke with a start, falling against the wheel, That circled slow after the sleepy horse. Yet none would yield to soft-suggesting sleep,

Or leave the last few shocks; for the wild storm Would catch thereby the skirts of Harvest-home, And hold her lingering half-way in the rain.

The scholar laboured with his men all night. He did not favour such prone headlong race With Nature. To himself he said : " The night Is sent for sleep, we ought to sleep in it, And leave the clouds to God. Not every storm That climbeth heavenward, overwhelms the earth. And if God wills, 'tis better as he wills ; What he takes from us never can be lost." But the old farmer ordered ; and the son Went manful to the work, and held his peace.

When the dawn blotted pale the clouded east, And the first drops, o'ergrown and helpless, fell, Oppressed with sheaves, the last cart home was

going;

And by its side, the last in the retreat, The scholar walked, glad bringing up the rear.

Half distance only had he measured back,

When, on opposing strength of upper winds

Tumultuous borne at last, the labouring racks

Met in the zenith, and the silence ceased :

The lightning brake, and flooded all the world,

Its roar of airy billows following it.

The darkness drank the lightning, and again

Lay more unslaked. But ere the darkness came,

In the full revelation of the flash,

Met by some stranger flash from cloudy brain,

He saw the lady, borne upon her horse,

Careless of thunder, as when, years agone,

He saw her once, to see for evermore.

"Ah ha!" he said; "my dreams are come for me ;

Now shall they have their time." For, all the

night,

He had felt a growing trouble in his frame, Which might be nothing, or an illness dire. Homeward he went, with a pale smile arrived,

Gave up his load, walked softly to his room, And sought the welcome haven of his bed— There slept and moaned, cried out, and woke, and

slept:

Through all the netted labyrinth of his brain The fever shot its pent malignant fire. 'Twas evening when to passing consciousness He woke and saw his father by his side. His guardian form in every vision drear That followed, watching shone; and the healing

face

Of his good sister gleamed through all his pain, Soothing and strengthening with cloudy hope j Till, at the weary last of many days, He woke to sweet quiescent consciousness, Enfeebled much, but with a new-born life— His soul a summer evening, after rain.

Slow, with the passing weeks, he gathered strength,

And ere the winter came, seemed half-restored; And hope was busy. But a fire too keen Burned in his larger eyes ; and in his cheek Too ready came the blood at faintest call, Glowing a fair, quick-fading, sunset hue.

Before its hour, a biting frost set in. It gnawed with icy fangs his shrinking life ; And that disease well known in all the land, That smiling, hoping, wasting, radiant death, Was born of outer cold and inner heat.

One morn his sister, entering while he slept, Saw in his listless hand a handkerchief Spotted with red. Cold with dismay, she stood Soared, motionless. But catching in a glass A sudden glimpse of a white ghostly face, She started at herself, and he awoke. He understood, and said with smile unsure, " Bright red was evermore my master-hue ; And see, I have it in me : that is why."

She shuddered ; and he saw, nor jested more ; But from that hour looked silent Death in the

face.

When first he saw the red blood outward leap, As if it sought again the fountain-heart Whence it had flowed to fill the golden bowl, No terror seized—a wild excitement swelled His spirit. Now the pondered mystery Would fling its portals wide, and take him in, One of the awful dead : them fools conceive As ghosts that fleet and pine, bereft of weight, And half their valued lives—he otherwise ;

Hoped now, and now expected; and again Said only, " I will wait for what will come." So waits a child the lingering curtain's rise, While yet the panting lights restrained burn At half height, and the theatre is full. But as the days went on, they brought sag hours,

VOL. I. V

When he would sit, his hands upon his knees,
Drooping, and longing for the wine of life.
For when the ninefold crystal spheres, through
which

The outer light sinks in, are rent and shattered, Yet whole enough to keep the pining life, Distressing shadows cross the chequered soul : Poor Psyche trims her irresponsive lamp, A.nd anxious visits oft her store of oil, A.nd still the shadows fall—she must go pray. For God, who speaks to man at door and lattice, Glorious in stars, and winds, and flowers, and

waves,

Not seldom shuts the door and dims the pane, That, isled in calm, his still small voice may sound The clearer, by the hearth, in the inner room— Sound on until the soul, fulfilled of hope, Look undismayed on that which cannot kill; And saying in th«» gloom, I will the lighi.

Glow in the gloom the present will of God— So melt the shadows of her clouded house.

He, when his lamp shot up a spiring flame, Would thus break forth and climb the heaven of

prayer.

" Do with us what thou wilt, all-glorious heart! Thou God of them that are not yet, but grow ! We trust thee for the thing we shall be yet; We too are ill content with what we are." And when the flame sank, and the darkness fell, He lived by faith which is the soul of sight.

Yet in the frequent pauses of the light, When all was dreary as a drizzling thaw, When sleep came not although he prayed for sleep, And wakeful weary on his bed he lay, Like frozen lake that has no heaven within; Then, then the sleeping horror woke and stirred, And with the tooth of unsure thought began To gnaw the roots of life. What if there wer*

V 2

No truth in beauty—loveliness a toy
Invented by himself in happier mood ?
" For, if my mind can dim or slay the Fair,
Why should it not enhance or make the Fair ? "
" Nay," Psyche answered ; " for a tired man
May drop his eyelids on the visible world,
To whom no dreams, when fancy flieth free,
Will bring the sunny excellence of day.
'Tis easy to destroy; God only makes.
Could my invention sweep the lucid waves
With purple shadows—next create the joy

With which my life beholds them? Wherefore
should
One meet the other without thought of mine? If God did not mean beauty in them and me,
But dropped them, helpless shadows, from his
sun,
There were no God, his image not being mine, And I should seek in vain for any bliss.
Oh, lack and doubt and fear can only come Because of plenty, confidence, and love ! They are the shadow-forms about their feet, Because they are not perfect crystal-clear To the all-searching sun in which they live. Dread of its loss is Beauty's certain seal!" Thus reasoned mourning Psyche. And suddenly The sun would rise, and vanish Psyche's lamp, Absorbed in light, not swallowed in the dàrk.

It was a wintry time with sunny days, And visitings of April airs and scents, That came with sudden presence, unforetold, As brushed from off the outer spheres of spring In the great world where all is old and new. Strange longings he had never known till now, Awoke within him, flowers of rooted hope. For a whole silent hour he would sit and gaze Upon the distant hills whose dazzling snow Starred the dim blue, or down their dark ravine?

Crept vaporous; until the fancy rose That on the other side those rampart hills, A mighty woman sat, with waiting face, Calm as the life whose rapt intensity Borders on death, silent, waiting for him, To make him grand for ever with a kiss, And send him silent through the toning worlds. The father saw him waning. The proud sire Beheld his pride go drooping in the cold, Like snowdrop to the earth; and gave God
thanks
That he was old. But evermore the son Looked up and smiled as he had heard strange
news,
Across the waste, of tree-buds and primroses. And yet again the other mood would come, And, being a troubled child, he sought his father For comfort such as fathers only give :— bure there is one great Father in the heavens,
Since every word of good from fathers' lips
Falleth with such authority, although
They are but men as we ! This trembling son
Who saw the unknown death draw hourly nigher,
Sought comfort in his father's tenderness,
And made him strong to die.
One shining day,
Shining with sun and snow, he came and said, " What think you, father—is death very sore ? " " My boy," the father answered, " we will try To make it easy with the present God. But, as I judge, though more by hope than sight, It seems much harder to the lookers on, Than to the man who dies. Each panting breath, We call a gasp, may be to him who knows, A sigh of pleasure ; or, at worst, the sob With which the unclothed spirit, step by step, Wades forth into the cool eternal sea. I think, my boy, death has two sides to it—
One sunny, and one dark j as this round earth
Is every day half sunny and half dark.
We on the dark side call the mystery death;
They on the other, looking down in light,
Wait the glad birth, with other tears than ours.
" Be near me, father, when I die; " he said.

" I will, my boy, until a better father
Draws your hand out of mine. Be near in turn,
When my time comes—you in the light beyond.
And knowing all about it—I all dark."
The days went on, until the tender green Shone through the snow in patches. Then tne hope
Of life awoke, fair-faintly, in his heart; For the spring drew him, warm, soft, budding spring, With promises. The father better knew.
He who had strode a king across his fields, Crept slowly now through softest daisied grass ;
And sometimes wept in secret, that so soon The earth with all its suns and harvests fail- Must lie beyond a sure-dividing waste.
But though I lingering listcn to the old, Ere yet I strike new chords that seize the old And bear their lost souls up the music-stair— Think not he was too fearful-faint of heart To look the blank unknown full in the void ; For he had hope in God, the growth of years, Ponderings, and aspirations from a child, And prayers and readings and repentances; For something in him had ever sought the peace Of other something deeper in him still; Some sounds sighed ever for a harmony With other fainter tones, that softly drew Nearer and nearer from the unknown depths Where the Individual goeth out in God, Smoothing the discord ever as they grew : He sought the way back which the music came.
Hoping at last to find the face of him
To whom St. John said Lord with holy awe,
Yet on his bosom fearless leaned the while.
As the slow spring came on, his swelling life, The new creation inside of the old, Pressed up in buds toward the invisible, And burst the crumbling mould wherein it lay. He never thought of churchyards, ever looked Away from the green earth to the blue sky.
Yet of the earth remained one hurtless stain— He thanked God that he died not in the cold. " For," said he, " I would rather go abroad When the sun shines, and birds are singing blithe.
It may be that we know not any place, Or sense at all, and only live in thought, But, knowing not, I cling to warmth and light, I may pass forth into the sea of air That swings its massy waves around the earth,
And I would rather go when it is full
Of light and blue and larks, than when gray fog
Dulls it with steams of old earth winter-sick.
Now in the dawn of summer I shall die ;
Sinking asleep at sunset, I will hope,
And going with the light. And by the time
When they say: ' He is dead; his face is changed;'
I shall be saying : ' Yet, yet, I live, I love."
The weary nights had taught him much; for all He knew before seemed as he knew it not, And he must learn it yet again and better. The sick half-dreaming child will oft forget In longings for his mother, that her arms Are all the time holding him to her heart: Mother he murmuring moans ; she wakes him up That he may see her face, and sleep in peace. And God was very good to him, he said.
Faint-hearted reader, lift thy heart with me.— Father ! we need thy winter as thy spring;

And thy poor children, knowing thy great heart, And that thou bearest thy large share of grief, Because thou lovest goodness more than joy In them thou lovest—so dost let them grieve, Will cease to vex thee with our peevish cries, Will lift our eyes and smile, though sorrowful; Yet not the less pray for thy help, when pain Is overstrong. Remember our poor hearts. We never grasp the zenith of the time; We find no spring except in winter-prayers ; But we believe—nay, Lord, we only hope, That one day we shall thank thee perfectly For pain and hope and all that led or drove Us back into the bosom of thy love.

One night, as oft, he lay and could not sleep. His spirit was a chamber, empty, dark, Through which bright pictures passed of the outer

world; The regnant Will gazed passive on the show.

The tube, as it were, through which the shadows

came,

Was turned upon the past. One after one, Glided across the field the things that were, Silent and sorrowful, like all things old ; For withered rose-leaves have a mournful scent, And old brown letters are more sad than graves.

At length, as ever in such vision-hours, Came the bright maiden, high upon her horse. Then, then the passive Will sprang regnant up, And, like a necromantic sage, compelled What came unbidden to abide his will.

Gathered around her form his brooding thoughts: How would she fare, spinning her history Into a psyche-cradle ? With what wings Greet the feonian summer ? Glistening white, With feathery dust of silver ? or dull red, Seared with black spots of scorching sulphur-fume?

"I know," he said, " some women fail, and cease. Men rave of eyes in which I could not rest."

The fount of possibilities began To glow ebullient in the hidden part; Anon the lava-stream burst blasting forth. For purest souls sometimes have direst fears, In ghost-hours when the shadow of the earth Is cast on half her children, and the sun Is far away and busy with the rest. " If she be only such as some men say, Pure in the eyes of poet-boys, who still Fancy the wavings of invisible wings, And tremble as they feel the wafted air; But, private and familiar with their thoughts, Common as clay, and of the trodden earth ! It cannot, cannot be ! She is of God. And yet fair things will perish ; higher life Gives deeper death ; fair gifts make fouler faults : Women themselves—I dare not think the rest."

Such thoughts went walking up and down his soul, Until they found a spot wherein to rest, And build a resolution for the day.

But next day, and the next, he was too worn To make intent a deed. Besides, there blew A cold dry wind from out the kindless east, Withering his life—as if he had come too soon, Before God's spirit moved on the waters' face, To make his dwelling ready. But the next Morning rose radiant. A genial wind Rippled the blue air 'neath the golden sun, And brought glad news of summer from the south

He lay now in his father's room ; and there The growing summer sun poured a steep light. It fell upon the fire, alive with flames, And turned it ghostly pale, and would have slain , Even as the sunshine of the further life, Quenching the glow of this, leaves but a coal. He sat him down 'twixt sun and fire, himself

A HIDDEN LIFE.

The meeting point of two conflicting lives,
And half from each forth flowed the written
stream.

"Lady, I owe thee much. Stay not to look Upon my name : I write it, but I date From the churchyard, where it shall lie in peace When thou art reading—and thou know'st me

not.

Nor dared I write, but death is crowning me Thy equal. If my boldness should offend, I, pure in my intent, hide with the ghosts ; Where when thou com'st, thou hast already known, As God at first, Death equal makes at last.

But pardon, lady. Ere I had begun, My thoughts moved towards thee with a gentle

flow

That bore a depth of waters. When I took My pen to write, they rushed into a gulf, Precipitate and foamy. Can it be,

That death who humbles all hath made me

proud ?

Lady, thy loveliness hath walked my brain, As if I were thy heritage bequeathed From many sires ; yet only from afar I have worshipped thee—content to know the

vision

Had lifted me above myself who saw, And ta'en my angel nigh thee in thy heaven. Thy beauty, lady, hath overflowed, and made Another being beautiful beside With virtue to aspire and be itself. Afar as angels or the sainted dead, Yet near as loveliness can haunt a man, And taking any shape for every need, Thy form hath put on each revealing dress Of circumstance and history, high or low, In which from tale of holy life and thought Essential womanhood hath shone on me.

Ten years have passed away since the first time Which was the last, I saw thee. What have

these Made or unmade in thee ? I ask myself.

0 lovely in my memory ! art thou

As lovely in thyself? Thy glory then

Was what God made thee : art thou such indeed

Forgive my boldness, lady—I am dead :

The dead may cry, their voices are so small.

I have a prayer to make thee—hear the dead. Lady, for God's sake be as beautiful As that white form that dwelleth in my heart ; Yea, better still, as that ideal Pure That waketh in thee, when thou prayest God, Or helpest thy poor neighbour. For myself

1 pray. For if I die and find that she, My woman-glory, lives in common air, f s not so very radiant after all,

My sad face will afflict the calm-eyed ghosts,

A HIDDEN LIFE ,

Unused to see such rooted sadness there.

With palm to palm, my kneeling ghost implores

Thee, living lady—justify my faith

In womanhood's white-handed nobleness,

And thee, its revelation unto me.

But I bethink me. If thou turn thy thoughts Upon thyself, even for that great sake Of purity and conscious whiteness' self, Thou wilt but half succeed. The other half Is to forget the first, and all thyself, Quenching thy moonlight in the blaze of day, Turning thy being full unto thy God. Be thou in him a pure, twice holy child, Doing the rigtt with sweet unconsciousness j Having God in thee, thy completed soul.

Lady, I die—the Father holds me up. It is not much to thee that I sho' .Id die ; But it is much to know He hold me up.

I thank thee, lady, for a gent" 2 look

Which crowned me from thine eyes ten years Ere, clothed in nimbus of the setting sun, Thee from my dazzled eyes thy horse did bear, Proud of his burden. My dull tongue was mute— I was a fool before thee; but my silence Was the sole homage possible to me then : That I can speak nor be ashamed, is thine. The same sweet look be possible to thee For evermore—I bless thee with thine own, And say farewell, and go into my grave— Nay, to the sapphire heaven of all my hopes."

Followed his name in full, and then the name Of the green churchyard where his form would lie.

Back to his couch he crept, weary, and said : " O God ! I am but an attempt at life. Sleep falls again ere I am full awake. Life goeth from me in the morning hour. I have seen nothing clearly; felt no thrill Hf rsiire e«iQt ; on, save in dreams, ah—dreams

The high Truth has but flickered in my soul— Save at such times, in lonely midnight hours, When, dawning sudden on my inner world, New stars came forth, revealing unknown depths, New heights of silence, quelling all my sea. Then only I beheld the formless fact, Beheld myself a living lonely thought, Isled in the hyaline of Truth alway. I have not reaped earth's harvest, O my God; Have gathered but a few poor wayside flowers, Harebells, red poppies, daisies, eyebrights blue-Gathered them by the way, for comforting. Have I aimed proudly, therefore aimed too Icrv, Striving for something visible in my thought, And not the unseen thing hid far in thine V Make me content to be a primrose-flower Among thy nations, so the fair truth, hid In the sweet primrose, come awake in nw, And I rejoice, an individual soul,

Reflecting tliee—as truly then divine
As if I towered the angel of the sun.
Once, in a southern eve, a glowing worm
Gave me a keener joy than the heaven of stars :
Thou earnest in the worm more near me then;
Nor do I think, were I that green delight,
I'd change to be the shadowy evening star.
Ah, make me, Father, anything thou wilt,
So be thou will it! I am safe with thee.
I laugh exulting. Make me something, God ;
Clear, sunny, veritable purity
Of high existence, in thyself content,
And seeking for no measures. I have reaped
Earth's harvest, if I find this holy death.
Now I am ready ; take me when thou wilt."

He laid the letter in his desk, with seal And superscription. When his sister came, He told her where to find it— afterwards.

cne slow eve, through paler, darker shades.
A HIDDEN LIFE.
Insensibly declines, until at last
Thd iordly day is but a memory,
So died he. In the hush of noon he died.
The sun shone on—why should he not shine on ?

The summer noises rose o'er all the land.
The love of God lay warm on hill and plain.
'Tis well to die in summer.
When the breath,

After a hopeless pause, returned no more, The father fell upon his knees, and said : " O God, I thank thee ; it is over now ; Through this sore time thy hand has led him well. Lord, let me follow soon, and be at rest." And then he rose, and comforted the maid, Who in her brother had lost the pride of life, And wept as all her heaven were only rain.

Of the loved lady, little more I know. I know not if. when she had read the lines, She rose in haste, and to her chamber went,

A HIDDEN LIFE.
And shut the door; nor if, when she came forth,
A dawn of holier purpose gleamed across-
The sadness of her brow. But this I know,
That on a warm autumnal afternoon,
When headstone-shadows crossed three neighbour
graves,

And, like an ended prayer, the empty church Stood in the sunshine, like a cenotapa, A little boy, who watched a cow near by Gather her milk where alms of clover-fields Lay scattered on the sides of silent roads, All sudden saw—but saw not whence she came— A lady, closely veiled, alone, and still, Seated upon a grave. Long time she sat And moved not, weeping sore, the watcher said. At length slow-leaning on her elbow down, She pulled a something small from off the grave— A shining daisy, or a blade of grass, And put it in a letter. Then she rose,

A HIDDEN LIFE.
And glided silent forth, over the wall, Where the two steps on this side and on that Shorten the path from westward to the church. The clang of hoofs and sound of light, swift wheels Arose and died upon the listener's ear.

THE END

CPSIA information can be obtained
at www.ICGtesting.com
Printed in the USA
LVHW061558271219
641885LV00014B/464/P

9 781543 067149